Macmillan
Animal
Encyclo-
pedia
for
Children

Ostrich

Gavial

Previous page: Otter
Facing page: Eclectus parrots

Macmillan
Animal Encyclo-pedia
for
Children

ROGER FEW

Macmillan Publishing Company New York

Maxwell Macmillan Canada Toronto

Maxwell Macmillan International Publishing Group
New York Oxford Singapore Sydney

A Marshall Edition
This book was conceived, edited and designed by
Marshall Editions Limited, 170 Piccadilly,
London W1V 9DD

Macmillan Publishing Company is part of the Maxwell
Communication Group of Companies.

Macmillan Publishing Company
866 Third Avenue
New York, NY 10022

Maxwell Macmillan Canada, Inc.
1200 Eglinton Avenue East
Suite 200
Don Mills, Ontario M3C 3N1

**All photographs supplied by
Oxford Scientific Films**

Film supplied by Dorchester Typesetting Group Limited
and Pressdata

Origination by Chroma Graphics, Singapore

Printed and bound in Spain by Printer Industria Gráfica SA,
Barcelona

First American edition
10 9 8 7 6 5 4 3 2

Library of Congress Cataloging-in-Publication Data
is available

ISBN 0-02-762425-0

CONTENTS

6   Introduction

8   ICE CAPS AND TUNDRA
10   Life on the ice caps and tundra
12   Birds and mammals
14   Focus on: The Siberian tundra

16   CONIFEROUS FORESTS
18   Life in the coniferous forests
20   Mammals
22   Focus on: Canadian coniferous forest
24   Birds

26   WOODLANDS
28   Life in the woodlands
30   Mammals
32   Focus on: Australian eucalyptus woodland
34   Birds
36   Reptiles and amphibians

38   GRASSLANDS
40   Life on the grasslands
42   Mammals
44   Focus on: East African savanna
46   Birds
48   Reptiles and amphibians

Galapagos giant tortoise

50 DESERTS
52 Life in the deserts
54 Mammals
56 Focus on: The American Southwest
58 Birds
60 Reptiles and amphibians

62 TROPICAL FORESTS
64 Life in the tropical forests
66 Mammals
68 Focus on: The Amazon rainforest
70 Mammals
72 Birds
74 Reptiles and amphibians

76 MOUNTAINS
78 Life in the mountains
80 Birds and mammals
82 Focus on: The Himalayas

84 RIVERS AND LAKES
86 Life in rivers and lakes
88 Mammals
90 Focus on: A European river
92 Birds
94 Reptiles and amphibians
96 Fishes

98 OCEANS
100 Life in the oceans
102 Mammals
104 Birds
106 Focus on: Pacific deep sea
108 Reptiles and fishes
110 Fishes
112 Focus on: Great Barrier Reef
114 Fishes

116 Glossary
117 Index
120 Acknowledgments

Red kangaroo

INTRODUCTION

Humans divide the world into countries. Nature divides it into areas according to how hot, cold, wet, or dry they are and what plants grow there. These natural areas are the Earth's habitats and include tundra, forest, woodland, and desert. Every habitat is different because of its climate and the sorts of plants that can live there. It may be hot and dry with few plants, as in the desert, or hot and very wet with an enormous variety of plants, as in the tropical rainforest.

The plant life in turn determines the kinds of animals that live in a habitat. Some creatures feed directly on the plants themselves. Others hunt and feed on the plant-eaters. All kinds of animals use plants for shelter and as places to build nests or homes. In addition to the land habitats there are the freshwater and ocean kingdoms with their own special inhabitants.

Each animal is designed for life in a particular habitat. Many woodland creatures are good climbers and have special paws and tails that help them hold onto tree branches. Grassland animals are fast runners. Fish are adapted to live and breathe in water.

Taking as a starting point the fact that every animal has its place in the world, this encyclopedia selects the planet's major natural habitats and looks at the creatures that live there.

In each chapter the habitat is first described and illustrated by a color photograph. The following pages then look at the habitat in more detail. A map shows

Golden lion tamarin

where in the world it is found. Rainfall and temperature diagrams show the climate of one particular place. A selection of animals that are well adapted to that habitat give an idea of life there.

Illustrated "catalogs" of some of the spectacular animals in each habitat follow. The size and scientific name of each are given, together with where it is found and a short description of its habits.

Within each habitat chapter, special "Focus on" features look at one particular place in that habitat in more detail—the African savanna, the Amazon rainforest, the Himalayas, for example. Each is illustrated by an artist's impression of the landscape, including a selection of typical animals.

Looking at the natural order of nature in this way helps us understand the fascinating world of animals. It explains how so many different kinds of animals can survive by showing how they all fit into their different habitats and ways of life.

And understanding the wonders of nature is more important now, when so many creatures are under threat, than ever before. Animals are hunted and killed for their horns, their skins, and their flesh. Forests are being destroyed, oceans polluted. Many of the habitats described here and the vast range of animals that live in them could disappear for ever. Their future depends on us, and understanding the natural world is the first step toward ensuring its survival.

Ocean sunfish

Ice caps and tundra

The coldest, loneliest parts of the world where the few animals and plants struggle to survive the harsh conditions

The polar regions at the ends of the Earth are bitterly cold. In these places the snow never melts and the sea is always covered with ice. Even the pattern of day and night is strange. In midsummer, the sun shines 24 hours a day. In winter, there is complete darkness for months on end.

The region that surrounds the North Pole is called the Arctic. Most of the Arctic is sea, but at its center there is a huge area of floating ice, nearly 2,000 miles across. This is called "pack ice."

The Arctic Ocean is almost completely surrounded by land. This includes the northern parts of Europe, Asia, and North America, as well as Greenland and Iceland. Greenland is covered with a thick sheet of ice all year round, but most of the Arctic lands are not iced over. Instead they have bare rocks and scattered plants. This bleak, treeless landscape is known as "tundra."

During summer there is just enough sunshine in the tundra areas to thaw the top layers of soil and allow plants to grow. The only plants that can survive the fierce winds that blow here are small and low-growing and many lie flat against the ground.

The Antarctic, the region around the South Pole, is even colder than the Arctic. Instead of ice-covered sea, it has the continent of Antarctica at its center. A layer of ice nearly 2 miles thick covers the continent and spills over its coasts into the surrounding ocean.

The few plants that live on Antarctica are mainly lichens and mosses that grow on bare rocks. Farther out to sea, there are slightly warmer, rocky islands, where short plants can grow. But because there are only small islands around the southern ice cap, the Antarctic has no great regions of tundra.

Dwarfed by towering icy cliffs, a colony of emperor penguins enjoys the brief Antarctic summer.

Life on the ice caps and tundra

Very few animals live on the ice caps all the time, but Antarctica has some tiny insects and mites that feed among the mosses and lichens on the ground.

In the seas around both poles, though, there are plenty of fish and other sea creatures. These provide food for seabirds and for mammals such as polar bears and seals that come to rest or breed on the ice. These animals have thick fur to protect them from the bitter cold.

In winter, the tundra is also a lonely place. A few small mammals such as lemmings and voles search for seeds and grass, often digging beneath the snow to find them. They can shelter from the icy wind in burrows, but larger mammals such as musk ox and caribou have nowhere to hide.

But when the brief summer comes, the tundra changes

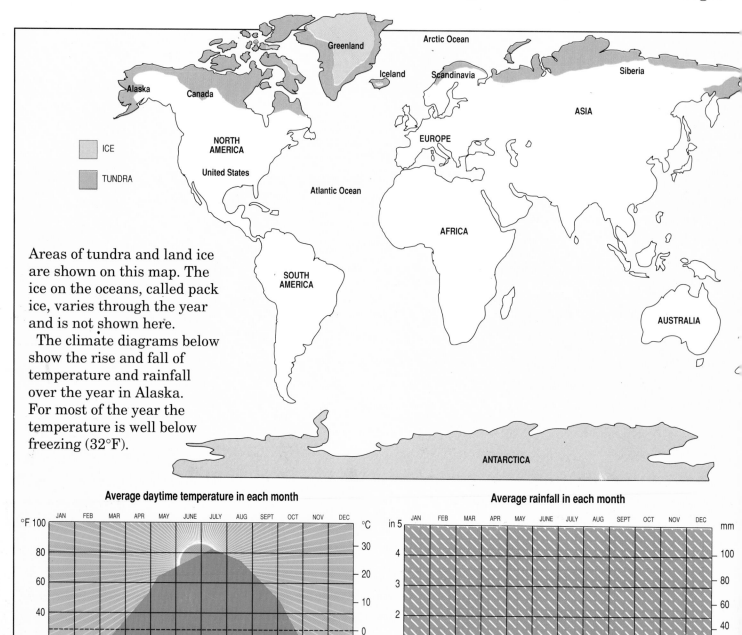

Areas of tundra and land ice are shown on this map. The ice on the oceans, called pack ice, varies through the year and is not shown here.

The climate diagrams below show the rise and fall of temperature and rainfall over the year in Alaska. For most of the year the temperature is well below freezing (32°F).

Average daytime temperature in each month

Average rainfall in each month

dramatically. As the snow melts and the ground thaws, new green growth appears on plants, and flowers open.

The white camouflage worn by several birds and mammals is no longer so useful. Some molt their old feathers or fur to become brown in color.

Polar bear

ARCTIC COASTS

A thick creamy-white coat keeps the polar bear warm in winter and helps it hide from its prey. It runs fast, even on ice, and swims well.

Snowy owl

ARCTIC COASTS

This owl hunts lemmings and any other small animals and birds it can find in its snowy home. Unlike most owls it will hunt in daylight.

Emperor penguin

ANTARCTIC OCEAN

Although penguins cannot fly, they are good swimmers and hunt fish and squid underwater. Their thick waterproof feathers keep them warm in the cold sea.

Walrus

ARCTIC OCEAN

Ideally suited to life in the Arctic, walruses swim well and can push themselves along on ice with their flippers. They feed on shellfish, which are plentiful in the Arctic.

Musk ox

NORTHERN CANADA, GREENLAND

Thick fur under an outer layer of long coarse hair protects the musk ox from cold and wet. Broad hooves keep it from sinking into soft snow.

Ivory gull

Norway lemming

FOUND IN:
Scandinavia

SIZE:
body 6 in; tail ¾ in

SCIENTIFIC NAME:
Lemmus lemmus

A busy little rodent, the Norway lemming feeds on grasses, shrubs, and mosses. In winter, it clears runways under the snow so that it can search for food.

This plump-bodied bird is the only all-white gull. It nests in large colonies on lonely islands.

FOUND IN:
Arctic coasts and islands

SIZE:
16-18 in

SCIENTIFIC NAME:
Pagophila eburnea

Dovekie

FOUND IN:
North Atlantic and Arctic oceans

SIZE:
8-10 in

SCIENTIFIC NAME:
Alle alle

The dovekie, or little auk, is a stout bird with short wings and a strong bill. It is a good swimmer and feeds on small fish and other sea creatures.

Leopard seal

FOUND IN:
Antarctic pack ice and islands

SIZE:
9-11 ft

SCIENTIFIC NAME:
Hydrurga leptonyx

The leopard seal, with its slender, streamlined body, can move fast. It is the fiercest hunter of all seals and preys on penguins which it catches underwater in its large, tooth-studded jaws. It also hunts other smaller seals, as well as fish and squid.

Caribou

FOUND IN:
**Northern Europe and Asia,
Alaska, Canada, Greenland**

SIZE:
body 4-7½ ft; tail 4-8 in

SCIENTIFIC NAME:
Rangifer tarandus

The caribou, also known as the reindeer, is the only deer in which both male and female have antlers. In winter, caribou feed mainly on lichens. In summer, they travel north to feed on the rich grass and plants of the tundra.

Snowy sheathbill

These birds are eager scavengers of any food they can find. They haunt penguin colonies to seize eggs and chicks, and search the garbage dumps of Antarctic research stations. Sheathbills also feed on fish.

FOUND IN:
**Antarctic coasts and
South Atlantic islands**

SIZE:
16 in

SCIENTIFIC NAME:
Chionis alba

Golden plover

In winter, this plover leaves its tundra breeding grounds and flies some 8,000 miles to the warmth of South America.

FOUND IN:
**Arctic North America (summer);
South America (winter)**

SIZE:
9-11 in

SCIENTIFIC NAME:
Pluvialis dominica

Wolverine

The burly wolverine is a powerful hunter and can kill animals larger than itself. It also feeds on insects, eggs, and berries.

FOUND IN:
Siberia, Scandinavia, northern North America

SIZE:
body 25-34 in; tail 6-10 in

SCIENTIFIC NAME:
Gulo gulo

Focus on: The Siberian tundra

The Siberian tundra stretches across the far north of the Soviet Union, crossing hills and wide, flat plains. Some parts are gravelly; others have thick soil that becomes waterlogged in summer when the ice trapped in the ground thaws.

The plants of the tundra are short and slow-growing. The dwarf willow, a common shrub, is less than 16 inches high.

The dark Siberian winter is extremely cold. Temperatures sometimes drop as low as -58°F. This is too chilly for cold-blooded animals like snakes and lizards. But some warm-blooded mammals and birds can survive the winter if they have enough food and can find shelter from the worst of the weather.

In summer the Siberian tundra is much warmer, up to 65°F, and there are plenty of fresh buds and flowers. The hum of insects fills the air and hundreds of tiny freshwater creatures fill the pools left by the melted snow.

With so much food around this is a good place for birds to come and have their young. Millions of nests appear on the tundra in the summer months.

Rock ptarmigan
In winter, this ground-living bird has white feathers to blend with the snow and act as camouflage. In summer, it has darker feathers.

Ermine
Like the ptarmigan, the ermine, or stoat, has a white coat in winter. Dar fur grows again in spring.

Whimbrel
The long-legged whimbrel breeds in the tundra. Birds arrive in the spring and make their nests on the open ground.

14

Arctic fox
Small mammals and birds are the prey of this fox. In winter, when food is scarce, it may follow polar bears to feed on the remains of their kills.

Gyrfalcon
A skillful hunter, this falcon preys on the many nesting birds in the tundra. It kills its prey by gripping it in its sharp talons.

Arctic hare
This large white hare stays on the tundra all year round, feeding on low-growing plants.

Tundra swan
These swans spend the winter south of the tundra. They return each summer to breed, usually to the same place.

Snow bunting
The plump little snow bunting sometimes burrows in the snow to escape the cold of the tundra.

15

Coniferous forests

Dark, mysterious forests of the far north where towering trees crowd closely together

South of the Arctic stand the world's biggest forests—the great coniferous forests of North America and northern Asia. Conditions here are extremely harsh. In winter, the forests may be even colder than the tundra, and thick snow lies piled up against tree trunks for months. When the ground is frozen, the trees cannot get any water through their roots and they are in danger of drying out.

The forests are known as "coniferous" because the trees that can survive there are the "conifers," mainly pine, larch, spruce, and fir trees. These trees grow their seeds in cones and have thin, needle-shaped leaves. Needle leaves are just right for this type of climate. Snow slides off them easily and they do not let out much moisture into the air. There is so little sap in a needle leaf that if it freezes little damage is caused.

Protected in this way, the tree can hold onto its leaves all through the winter. Such trees are called "evergreen." By keeping its leaves, the tree is able to grow again as soon as there is enough sunshine at the start of spring.

The tall forest trees cast so much shade that it is hard for other plants to grow around them. In dense fir and spruce forests, only a layer of old needles covers the ground.

Summer is short in these northern forests. From May to August, the trees are busy growing, flowering, and making seeds while there is still enough sunshine. Tender buds burst into growth and small flowers open. New green cones start to grow while the older brown cones of the year before spread open to let their seeds out.

A lone moose stops to search for food in a clearing in the dense Canadian forest.

Life in the coniferous forests

Life is easiest for animals in the coniferous forest in summer. Weather is warmer and there is plenty of fresh plant food. There are also many insects. Ants and beetles crawl among the fallen needles. Swarms of midges, mosquitoes, and blackflies fill the air.

Forest birds quickly begin nesting so that their young hatch when there is lots of food for them to eat. Some nip off tender plant buds; others dart about the trees hunting insects.

On the ground, small rodents, such as voles and lemmings, are busy searching for seeds, nuts, and other foods.

This is also the time for the hunters of the forest to have their babies. While birds and rodents are looking after their young, they must look out for owls, hawks, lynxes, and martens. They, too, have hungry mouths to feed.

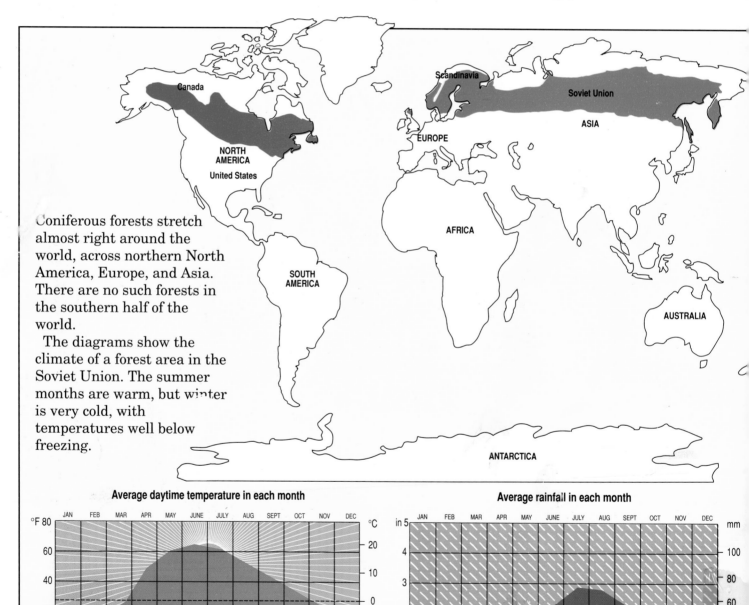

Coniferous forests stretch almost right around the world, across northern North America, Europe, and Asia. There are no such forests in the southern half of the world.

The diagrams show the climate of a forest area in the Soviet Union. The summer months are warm, but winter is very cold, with temperatures well below freezing.

Average daytime temperature in each month

Average rainfall in each month

Winter is a time of hardship. As the weather turns cold, fresh plants and insects become hard to find. Some animals try foods that are more difficult to eat. Forest deer often strip bark from trees with their teeth. Some birds may chew old pine needles.

Black woodpecker

EUROPE, ASIA

Using its strong beak, this bird drills into tree trunks to find ants and termites to eat.

Long-eared owl

NORTH AMERICA, EUROPE, ASIA

After a night of hunting small animals such as rats and mice, the long-eared owl roosts in a tall forest tree. Its speckled brown plumage helps it blend with its surroundings.

Crossbill

NORTH AMERICA, EUROPE, ASIA

Pine cone seeds are the crossbill's main food. It gets the seeds out with its special crossed beak.

Red squirrel

EUROPE, ASIA

In winter hungry squirrels use their sharp teeth to break into pine cones.

Brown bear

NORTH AMERICA, EUROPE, ASIA

After fattening up in summer, bears spend much of the winter asleep in their dens.

19

Beaver

Beavers eat leaves, bark, and twigs. They always live near water, and dam a stream to make a deep lake in which to hoard a winter food supply of branches.

FOUND IN:
North America

SIZE:
body 28-48 in; tail 8-11 in

SCIENTIFIC NAME:
Castor canadensis

Birch mouse

This rodent spends the day in its burrow and comes out at night to hunt for

insects and other tiny creatures to eat. It also feeds on seeds and fruit.

FOUND IN:
Northern Europe and Asia

SIZE:
body 2-3 in; tail 3-4 in

SCIENTIFIC NAME:
Sicista betulina

Lynx

Hares, rodents, and ground-living birds are the main prey of the stealthy lynx.

FOUND IN:
Europe, northern Asia, North America

SIZE:
body 31-48 in; tail 1-3 in

SCIENTIFIC NAME:
Felix lynx

Sable

An expert hunter, the sable catches rats, mice, and other small animals. It has long been hunted itself for its thick glossy fur and has become more and more rare in the wild.

FOUND IN:
Northern Asia

SIZE:
body 15-18 in; tail 5-7 in

SCIENTIFIC NAME:
Martes zibellina

Gray wolf

Wolves are powerful animals that live and hunt in family groups or packs. Together they can kill prey much larger than themselves, such as deer, caribou, and wild horses.

FOUND IN:
Europe, Asia, North America

SIZE:
body 3-4 ft; tail 11-18 in

SCIENTIFIC NAME:
Canis lupus

Snowshoe rabbit

A white winter coat helps this rabbit blend with the snows and hide from its enemies. In summer, when the snows melt, its fur turns dark brown.

FOUND IN:
Northern North America

SIZE:
body 14-20 in; tail 1-2 in

SCIENTIFIC NAME:
Lepus americanus

Woodchuck

In summer the woodchuck eats plenty of plant food and gets very fat. At the first sign of frost it goes into its burrow and sleeps through the winter, living on its store of body fat.

FOUND IN:
Northern North America

SIZE:
body 17-24 in; tail 7-9 in

SCIENTIFIC NAME:
Marmota monax

Focus on: *Canadian coniferous forest*

The coniferous forests of North America stretch from the freezing Arctic tundra south to the woodlands and prairies of the United States. Some of the most common trees in these huge forests are lodgepole pine, white spruce, balsam fir, and eastern larch.

Many of the biggest animals in North America live in coniferous forests. These forests are home to the moose and the caribou, which browse on forest plants. Bears also live in the forest and eat many kinds of foods.

Smaller mammals, such as lynxes, wolverines, and martens, are good at climbing as well as running. They can hunt in the trees as well as on the ground. Large birds, including the bald eagle and various types of hawk and owl, also hunt their prey here in the coniferous forest.

Red-breasted nuthatch
This nuthatch catches insects on the branches and trunks of conifers. It also eats cone seeds which it hoards as a winter food supply.

Black-capped chickadee
Always on the move, this chickadee hops nimbly over branches, searching for insects to eat.

Moose
In winter, moose shovel through the snow with their hooves to find mosses and lichens to eat.

Porcupine
Sharp-tipped spines on the porcupine's neck, back, and tail protect it from its enemies. It feeds on twigs, bark, and plant buds.

Many other birds that nest n the forest trees come rom farther south just for he summer. They fly north o feed their young on the nsects that appear among he trees in the warmer nonths. The birds' songs elp make the forest a much noisier place in summer.

Great horned owl
The forest provides plenty of prey for this nighttime hunter. It kills anything from insects to skunks and grouse.

Black bear
Like most bears, the black bear eats many different foods such as fruit, berries, and nuts as well as small animals.

Marten
An acrobatic animal with a bushy tail, the marten spends much of its time in trees, where it preys on squirrels.

Dark-eyed junco
A lively little bird, this junco feeds mostly on seeds but also catches insects and spiders in summer.

23

Goshawk

A powerful, fast-moving hunter, the goshawk kills prey with its strong talons. It hunts mice, rats, and rabbits, as well as birds such as pheasants and grouse. It may store large items of prey that it cannot finish in one meal.

FOUND IN:
North America, northern Europe, northern Asia

SIZE:
19-26 in

SCIENTIFIC NAME:
Accipiter gentilis

Red-flanked bluetail

This attractive little bird catches insects on the ground, its tail quivering as it moves.

FOUND IN:
Northern Asia

SIZE:
5½ in

SCIENTIFIC NAME:
Erithacus cyanurus

Hawk owl

Unlike most owls, this bird hunts in the day. It watches from a perch in a tree then swoops down on prey.

FOUND IN:
North America, northern Europe, northern Asia

SIZE:
14-15 in

SCIENTIFIC NAME:
Surnia ulula

Golden-crowned kinglet

The female kinglet builds a nest of moss, pine needles, and grass high in a conifer tree.

FOUND IN:
North America

SIZE:
3-4 in

SCIENTIFIC NAME:
Regulus satrapa

Pine grosbeak

The pine grosbeak eats fruit such as rowan berries, crushing them with its strong beak.

FOUND IN:
Northern North America, Scandinavia, northern Asia

SIZE:
8 in

SCIENTIFIC NAME:
Pinicola enucleator

Black grouse

FOUND IN:
Northern Europe and Asia

SIZE:
16-20 in

SCIENTIFIC NAME:
Tetrao tetrix

In spring, male black grouse perform a display to attract female birds. Every morning they gather at a special place to dance, call, and spread their beautiful tails before the watching females.

Western capercaillie

This magnificent, turkeylike bird feeds mainly on pine needles and seeds in winter. Its diet changes in summer when it eats the leaves and the juicy fruit of cranberry, bilberry, and other forest plants. The female bird is smaller than the male and has brownish feathers.

Female

Male

FOUND IN:
Northern Europe

SIZE:
male 34 in; female 23 in

SCIENTIFIC NAME:
Tetrao urogallus

Woodlands

From the rustling, sunlit treetops to the shady, leaf-strewn floor, the woodlands provide homes for many animals

In places where the weather is reasonably warm, most of the trees have a rounded shape, with branches spreading upward and outward. Their leaves are usually wide and flat, not like the needle leaves of fir trees and conifers. When these trees grow together in this gentler climate, they make what are called "temperate" woodlands.

In the patches of light and shade beneath the woodland trees, there may be a tangle of young trees and bushes, ferns, and small woodland flowers. This undergrowth is thickest in woods where there are wide spaces between the treetops for sunlight to shine through. Below this there is often a layer of dead leaves, twigs, rotting logs, mosses, and toadstools covering the woodland floor.

There are important differences between the various areas of temperate woodland in the world. Where the winters are quite cold, as in much of Europe and the United States, most of the woodland trees are "deciduous"—they lose their leaves in winter. The broad leaves of oak, elm, beech, hickory, and maple are ideally designed for catching sunlight during long, sunny summers.

But in winter they have little work to do and would probably be harmed by frost and strong winds. It is best for the leaves to wither and drop off in fall to be replaced by a new set of leaves in spring.

In southern Europe and parts of inland Australia, winters are warmer, but there is a long dry season every year, when little rain falls. Trees in these woods, such as olive, cork oak, and eucalyptus, are "evergreen"—they keep their leaves all year round. But these leaves are waxy and tough. They do not lose too much moisture in the dry air and help keep the trees alive even during long dry spells.

A pileated woodpecker perches by its nest hole, deep in a luxuriant New England woodland.

Life in the woodlands

In the woodlands there are many different places for animals to live.

Up in the treetops, there is a thick layer of leaves which forms the covering or "canopy" of the wood. Here there are lots of leaf-eating insects, especially caterpillars. The high branches make safe nesting places for many types of birds, which fill the air with their calls and songs. Small mammals, such as squirrels, also make their homes high in the trees.

On the shady woodland floor, big mammals such as deer take shelter and feed on leaves. Some woodland birds prefer to hide their nests low down in thickets. Among logs and tree roots there are plenty of hiding places for rodents, lizards, and snakes. Beneath them, the woodland soil is teeming with earthworms, beetles, and other insects which eat fallen

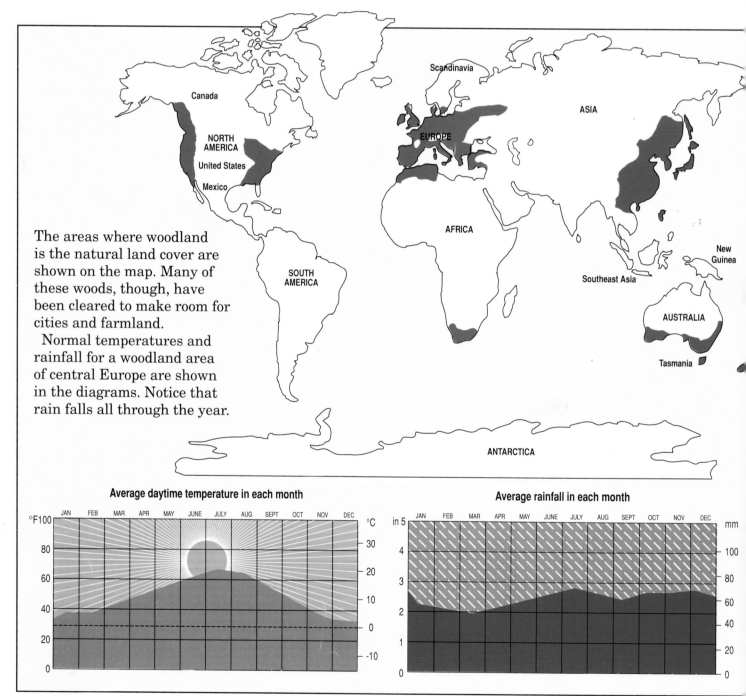

The areas where woodland is the natural land cover are shown on the map. Many of these woods, though, have been cleared to make room for cities and farmland.

Normal temperatures and rainfall for a woodland area of central Europe are shown in the diagrams. Notice that rain falls all through the year.

Average daytime temperature in each month

Average rainfall in each month

leaves and dead wood.
In cool climates, the woodland is not so busy in winter. The bare trees offer little shelter; there is no food for leaf-eaters and insects become scarce. Some animals hibernate—sleep through the winter. Many birds fly off to warmer areas.

Koala
AUSTRALIA
This animal spends most of its life in eucalyptus trees, where its long toes and claws give it a firm grip on the bark.

Yellow-bellied sapsucker
NORTH AMERICA
Using its strong beak, this woodpecker drills holes in trees and eats the sap that oozes out.

Eurasian badger
EUROPE, ASIA
A badger family makes its home in a network of burrows under the woodland floor.

Tawny owl
EUROPE, NORTH AFRICA, ASIA
Woodlands provide plenty of rodents and small birds for the tawny owl to hunt.

Gray squirrel
NORTH AMERICA
Sharp claws help this agile rodent scurry up and down the trees.

Red-backed salamander
UNITED STATES
Leaves and logs make hiding places for the salamander by day. At night it comes out to hunt for insects to eat.

29

White-tailed deer

FOUND IN:
**Southern Canada,
United States,
South America**

SIZE:
body 5-6 ft; tail 11in

SCIENTIFIC NAME:
*Odocoileus
virginianus*

Deer are usually the most common large animals in woodland. They eat many different types of food, including grasses, twigs, shrubby plants, nuts, and fungi. In the breeding season, male white-tailed deer compete in savage battles to win mates.

Eastern chipmunk

This bold rodent digs burrows under logs and rocks where it hides its stores of nuts and seeds.

FOUND IN:
**Southeast Canada and
eastern United States**

SIZE:
body 5-7 in; tail 3-4 in

SCIENTIFIC NAME:
Tamias striatus

Wood mouse

Seeds are the main food of this common woodland mouse, but it also eats nuts and berries.

FOUND IN:
Western Europe

SIZE:
body 3-5 in; tail 2-3 in

SCIENTIFIC NAME:
Apodemus sylvaticus

Masked shrew

Busy day and night, this shrew hunts insects, spiders, and snails on the woodland floor.

FOUND IN:
North America

SIZE:
body 2-4 in; tail 1-3 in

SCIENTIFIC NAME:
Sorex cinereus

Red fox

FOUND IN:
North America, Europe, Asia; introduced in Australia

SIZE:
body 18-33 in; tail 12-21 in

SCIENTIFIC NAME:
Vulpes vulpes

A skillful hunter, the red fox preys on many woodland creatures such as rats, mice, birds, and insects. It is most active at night and rests during the day in an underground burrow.

Wild boar

FOUND IN:
Europe, northwest Africa, Asia

SIZE:
body 3-4 ft; tail 6-8 in

SCIENTIFIC NAME:
Sus scrofa

The wild boar is the ancestor of the farmyard pig. With its long snout it roots around the woodland floor for plants and insects to eat. It also digs up bulbs and tubers.

Raccoon

FOUND IN:
North America

SIZE:
body 16-23 in; tail 7-16 in

SCIENTIFIC NAME:
Procyon lotor

The raccoon runs and climbs well and swims if necessary. It is most active at night and eats almost anything it can get hold of. As well as catching prey such as frogs, fish, mice, and birds, raccoons often raid garbage cans.

Wombat

In the heat of summer the burly wombat spends the day hidden in a deep burrow it digs below the woodland floor.

FOUND IN:
Eastern Australia and Tasmania

SIZE:
body 2-4 ft; tail 2 in

SCIENTIFIC NAME:
Vombatus ursinus

Focus on: *Australian eucalyptus woodland*

Parrots, koalas, giant lizards, deadly spiders—these are just some of the many animals that live in the woodlands of Australia. These woodlands are very different from those in Europe or North America. Many of the trees are gum trees, or eucalyptus. The leaves of these evergreen trees are stiff and waxy which stops them shriveling up in the scorching sun.

Many creatures depend on the trees of these woods for food and shelter. Leaf-eating insects such as caterpillars steadily munch their way through the foliage. Insects, bats, and birds feed on the sweet nectar of eucalyptus flowers. Colorful birds such as cockatoos and rosellas eat woodland fruits and berries.

Australia's famous marsupials are mammals which have pouches to protect their young while they are growing. Tree-living marsupials include possums, which eat a variety of plant foods, and koalas, which eat the leaves of eucalyptus trees.

Woodland hunters include darting birds, lizards, and spiders. In open woodland, the kookaburra bird pounces to snatch lizards and snakes, while the lace monitor, a huge lizard, climbs up trees to raid nests for eggs and young birds.

32

Carpet python
An agile climber, this snake hunts in trees and on the ground, killing birds and small animals such as mice and rabbits.

Brown antechinus
This marsupial searches for insect food up in eucalyptus trees.

Superb blue wren
Hopping about with its tail held up, this little bird searches for insects on the ground and on plants.

Sulfur-crested cockatoo
Seeds, fruit, nuts, flowers, and insects are the main foods of this cockatoo.

Brush-tailed possum
This marsupial feeds on leaves, fruit, and flowers, with some insects and young birds. It has become used to humans and will also eat food refuse.

Queensland blossom bat
Using its long brushlike tongue, this bat feeds on nectar and pollen from eucalyptus flowers.

Varied sittella
Much of the sittella's life is spent in trees, searching cracks in the bark for insects.

Greater glider
Steering itself with its long bushy tail, the greater glider can glide 300 feet or more from tree to tree.

Rainbow lory
Active, noisy birds, these lories fly around the trees, calling loudly and searching for food such as pollen, nectar, fruit, and leaves.

Superb lyrebird

Only the male lyrebird has the wonderful lyre-shaped tail. At mating time he spreads his shimmering tail and dances to attract female birds.

FOUND IN:
Australia

SIZE:
male 31-38 in; female 29-33 in

SCIENTIFIC NAME:
Menura novaehollandiae

Brown creeper

The brown creeper slowly climbs tree trunks, searching every crevice for insects.

FOUND IN:
North America, Europe, Asia

SIZE:
5-6 in

SCIENTIFIC NAME:
Certhia familiaris

Northern oriole

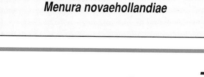

FOUND IN:
North America; winters in South America

SIZE:
6-7 in

SCIENTIFIC NAME:
Icterus galbula

The female oriole makes an unusual nest, which looks like a deep pouch. It is woven from grass, leaves, and other plant material and hangs from a twig.

Jay

The screech of the jay is a common sound in woodlands. This bird feeds on acorns and other nuts as well as on insects.

FOUND IN:
Europe, Asia, Southeast Asia

SIZE:
13 in

SCIENTIFIC NAME:
Garrulus glandarius

Cooper's hawk

An active hunter, this hawk chases other birds in the air or swoops on prey such as squirrels and chipmunks from a lookout perch. It even catches bats as they come out of caves.

FOUND IN:
North America

SIZE:
14-20 in

SCIENTIFIC NAME:
Accipiter cooperii

Great spotted woodpecker

FOUND IN:
Europe, North Africa, Asia

SIZE:
9 in

SCIENTIFIC NAME:
Picoides major

Using its strong, sharp bill, the woodpecker bores into tree trunks to find insects to eat. It also feeds on nuts, seeds, and berries.

Cardinal

FOUND IN:
North and Central America

SIZE:
8 in

SCIENTIFIC NAME:
Cardinalis cardinalis

Both male and female cardinals sing a variety of songs all year round. The female bird has brownish feathers, tinged with red.

American woodcock

The American woodcock feeds mainly on earthworms, which it finds by probing the soil with its long beak.

FOUND IN:
North America

SIZE:
11 in

SCIENTIFIC NAME:
Scolopax minor

35

Spring peeper

This agile frog can climb trees and jump more than 17 times its own body length.

FOUND IN:
North America

SIZE:
1 in

SCIENTIFIC NAME:
Hyla crucifer

Frilled lizard

FOUND IN:
Australia and New Guinea

SIZE:
body 9 in; tail 17 in

SCIENTIFIC NAME:
Chlamydosaurus kingii

If frightened, this lizard makes the frill of skin around its neck stick up. This warns off the enemy.

Wood turtle

This rough-shelled turtle stays near water but spends most of its life on land. It eats fruit, worms, and insects.

FOUND IN:
United States

SIZE:
5-9 in

SCIENTIFIC NAME:
Clemmys insculpta

Eastern coral snake

The colorful markings of this snake probably warn any enemies that it is poisonous.

FOUND IN:
United States and Mexico

SIZE:
22-48 in

SCIENTIFIC NAME:
Micrurus fulvius

Green anole

The male anole has a flap of pink skin on his throat. In the breeding season he fans this flap out in a display to attract females.

FOUND IN:
United States

SIZE:
4-7 in

SCIENTIFIC NAME:
Anolis carolinensis

Midwife toad

This toad has unusual breeding habits. After the female has laid her eggs, the male takes them and carries them on his back while they develop.

FOUND IN:
Western Europe

SIZE:
up to 2 in

SCIENTIFIC NAME:
Alytes obstetricans

Grass snake

The grass snake swims well and hunts fish and frogs in woodland rivers as well as mice on land. It is one of the commonest snakes in Europe.

FOUND IN:
Scandinavia, Europe, northwest Africa

SIZE:
up to 4 ft

SCIENTIFIC NAME:
Natrix natrix

Fire salamander

Bright markings warn that this salamander's body is covered with an unpleasant tasting slime. This puts off most hunters that might otherwise try to catch it. Although it spends most of its life on land it usually stays near water.

FOUND IN:
Europe, northwest Africa, parts of southwest Asia

SIZE:
8-11 in

SCIENTIFIC NAME:
Salamandra salamandra

37

Grasslands

Vast grassy plains where an amazing variety of animals and birds roam

Grass is extremely tough. It can stay alive in areas with scorching sunshine and little rain. It can spring up again after being burned by fire and can regrow after being chewed and trodden on by animals. Not surprisingly, grass is very plentiful in many parts of the world, especially in places where it is too dry for most trees to grow.

In gardens and fields grass is usually kept short by being cut or eaten. But in natural grassland the leaves of grass can be quite tall, more than 3 feet high. Each leaf is very thin, but because the plants grow closely together, they completely cover the ground. Underground, the grass roots make a dense tangle. This stops the soil blowing away, even if the leaves above have died and the earth has become very dry.

There are usually a few trees and bushes scattered across grassland. But these trees are hardy ones that can live through dry conditions. They may have long roots to find as much water as possible in the ground. Many have thick, leathery leaves that are good at keeping in water.

Changing seasons have different effects on the various grasslands of the world. On the prairies of North America and the steppes of Asia, there is plenty of fresh, green grass in spring and summer and many plants are in flower. They start to yellow in fall and, as the cold winter sets in, growth stops.

In tropical grasslands, such as the African savanna, the main problem is lack of water. Most growing and flowering happens in the rainy season. When the long dry season begins water becomes scarce. Old grass and other plants may become so dry at this time that fires start.

Herds of bison graze in Yellowstone National Park.

Life on the grasslands

Grassland is very different from woodland. It is much more open, with little shade or protection from the weather. Most of the food is near the ground, not high up.

Many insects, such as termites, ants, beetles, and grasshoppers, make their home on grassland. Most live low down in the grass where they are hard to spot.

Small mammals are common but are also difficult to see. Many grassland rodents, such as prairie dogs and ground squirrels, dig underground burrows. These are especially useful when the weather above ground is too hot or cold.

Grasslands are most famous for the big "herbivores"—antelopes, buffalo, elephants, and giraffes—that chew the plentiful grass and browse on the leaves of trees.

These plant-eating animals must be able to run fast.

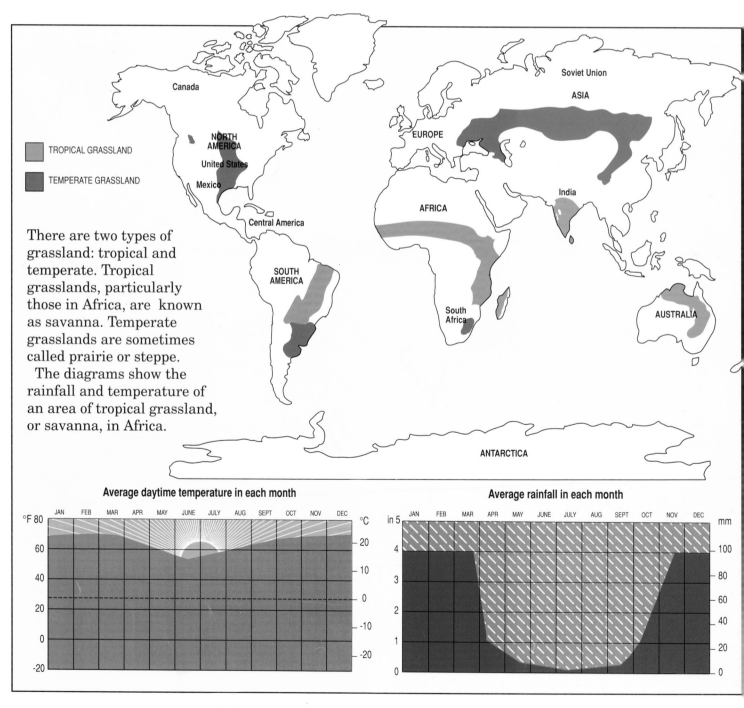

TROPICAL GRASSLAND

TEMPERATE GRASSLAND

There are two types of grassland: tropical and temperate. Tropical grasslands, particularly those in Africa, are known as savanna. Temperate grasslands are sometimes called prairie or steppe.

The diagrams show the rainfall and temperature of an area of tropical grassland, or savanna, in Africa.

Average daytime temperature in each month

Average rainfall in each month

There are few hiding places and running may be the only way they can escape from danger. But their enemies are also fast movers. Big cats, dogs, and foxes prowl the grasslands, and sharp-eyed hunting birds, such as hawks and eagles, watch for prey from the air.

Great bustard

EUROPE, ASIA

The world's heaviest flying bird, this bustard is also a fast runner.

Cheetah

AFRICA, ASIA

Long legs and a muscular body make the cheetah the fastest big cat.

Black-tailed jackrabbit

UNITED STATES

Strong hind limbs help the jackrabbit bound over the prairie in search of fresh green plants.

Giraffe

AFRICA

Standing nearly 20 feet high, the giraffe can feed on leaves and buds at the tops of savanna trees.

Leopard tortoise

AFRICA

Its hard, boldly patterned shell protects this tortoise from most enemies.

Giant anteater

CENTRAL AMERICA, SOUTH AMERICA

Using its strong claws, the anteater breaks open ant and termite nests and eats the insects inside.

41

Lion

The mighty lions hunt grassland mammals such as antelopes and zebras. They kill their prey with a swift bite to the neck. Lions live in groups called prides. A pride normally contains up to 3 males, 15 females, and their young.

FOUND IN:
Africa and northwest India

SIZE:
body 4-6½ ft; tail 26-39 in

SCIENTIFIC NAME:
Panthera leo

Common zebra

Herds of zebra roam the savanna, eating grass and sometimes leaves and bark.

FOUND IN:
Africa

SIZE:
body 6-7½ ft; tail 17-22 in

SCIENTIFIC NAME:
Equus burchelli

Saiga

FOUND IN:
Central Asia

SIZE:
body 4-5½ ft; tail 3-4 in

SCIENTIFIC NAME:
Saiga tatarica

In winter the saiga's coat grows thick and woolly to protect it from the bitter winds that blow on the steppe.

Maned wolf

FOUND IN:
South America

SIZE:
body 4 ft; tail 11 in

SCIENTIFIC NAME:
Chrysocyon brachyurus

A wary creature, the maned wolf hunts mainly at night. It preys on large rodents, birds, reptiles, and frogs.

American bison

FOUND IN:
North America

SIZE:
body 7-12 ft; tail 19-23 in

SCIENTIFIC NAME:
Bison bison

Once common on the American prairie, these magnificent animals are now only seen in national parks and reserves. They live in herds and feed on grass.

Black-tailed prairie dog

Prairie dogs live in huge underground burrows, called towns. A town may house several thousand animals.

FOUND IN:
Central United States

SIZE:
body 11-13 in; tail 3-4 in

SCIENTIFIC NAME:
Cynomys ludovicianus

Olive baboon

FOUND IN:
Africa

SIZE:
body up to 3 ft; tail 17-29 in

SCIENTIFIC NAME:
Papio anubis

Orderly troops of olive baboons move around the savanna, eating plants and fruit. They also hunt small animals such as young antelopes.

Black rhinoceros

The rhino's pointed, flexible upper lip helps it grab mouthfuls of leaves, buds, and shoots from small trees and bushes.

FOUND IN:
Africa

SIZE:
body 9-12 ft; tail 23-27 in

SCIENTIFIC NAME:
Diceros bicornis

Focus on: *East African savanna*

There are more kinds of large animals on the grassy plains of East Africa than anywhere else in the world. They include the biggest bird—the ostrich—and the tallest and heaviest land mammals—the giraffe and the African elephant.

In some wetter areas of the savanna, the grass is dense and tall, but in drier places it grows in low clumps. Some plains have lots of flat-topped acacia trees and strange baobab trees that store water in their thick trunks.

Not all the animals are competing for the same food. While giraffes chew the leaves at the top of trees, tiny dik-dik antelopes browse at the bottom of small bushes. Zebras nibble the tough ends of grass, but gazelles prefer the tender young shoots.

Other animals hunt for their food. Lions, leopards, cheetahs, hyenas, and hunting dogs are the biggest hunters. They can kill gazelles or even antelopes and zebras.

When the carnivores have finished eating, scavengers such as vultures and jackals often come along to seize the leftovers.

Impala
These graceful antelope move in herds of 200 or more, feeding on grass, leaves, and flowers.

Serval
This slender, long-legged cat is an expert grassland hunter.

Puff adder
A sluggish hunter, the puff adder lies in wait for small prey which it kills with its poisonous fangs.

Warthog
Using its strong tusks, the warthog digs in the ground for roots and bulbs.

Bateleur
Spectacular in the air, this long-winged eagle soars for hours at a time, searching for prey on the plains below.

Blue wildebeest
In the dry season, when food is scarce, huge herds of wildebeest walk hundreds of miles to find fresh grass.

African elephant
The elephant is the world's largest land-living animal. It eats about 350 pounds of food a day.

Helmeted guineafowl
Flocks of guineafowl roam the grassland, feeding on bulbs, roots, berries, and insects.

Plated lizard
This lizard lives in burrows, but comes out to hunt insects in the grass.

45

Ostrich

The ostrich is too big to fly but is so well designed for running that it is the fastest creature on two legs. It races across the grassland at up to 44 miles an hour.

FOUND IN:
Africa, mainly East and South Africa

SIZE:
6-9 ft tall

SCIENTIFIC NAME:
Struthio camelus

Burrowing owl

This little owl nests in burrows. It takes these over from prairie dogs or digs them for itself.

FOUND IN:
North, Central, and South America

SIZE:
7-10 in

SCIENTIFIC NAME:
Athene cunicularia

Red-billed quelea

In huge flocks of a million or more, queleas move like clouds across the sky.

FOUND IN:
Africa, south of the Sahara

SIZE:
4-5 in

SCIENTIFIC NAME:
Quelea quelea

Secretary bird

FOUND IN:
Africa, south of the Sahara

SIZE:
4-5 ft

SCIENTIFIC NAME:
Sagittarius serpentarius

This long-legged bird spends much of its life on the ground where it hunts snakes, birds, insects, and other small animals.

46

Red-legged seriema

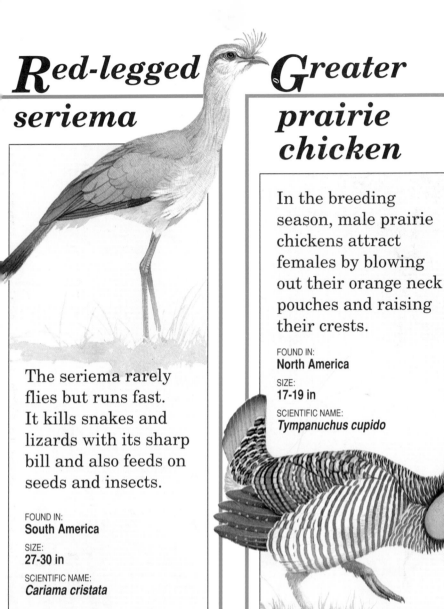

The seriema rarely flies but runs fast. It kills snakes and lizards with its sharp bill and also feeds on seeds and insects.

FOUND IN:
South America

SIZE:
27-30 in

SCIENTIFIC NAME:
Cariama cristata

Greater prairie chicken

In the breeding season, male prairie chickens attract females by blowing out their orange neck pouches and raising their crests.

FOUND IN:
North America

SIZE:
17-19 in

SCIENTIFIC NAME:
Tympanuchus cupido

Yellow-billed oxpecker

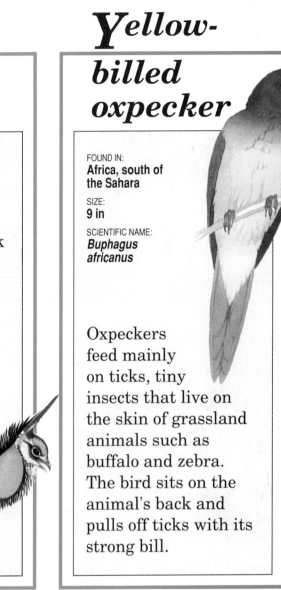

FOUND IN:
Africa, south of the Sahara

SIZE:
9 in

SCIENTIFIC NAME:
Buphagus africanus

Oxpeckers feed mainly on ticks, tiny insects that live on the skin of grassland animals such as buffalo and zebra. The bird sits on the animal's back and pulls off ticks with its strong bill.

Southern ground hornbill

FOUND IN:
Africa, south of the equator

SIZE:
35-51 in

SCIENTIFIC NAME:
Bucorvus cafer

Most hornbills live in trees, but this bird spends much of its life on the ground. It wanders around in pairs or family groups, searching for insects, reptiles, and other small animals to eat.

47

Great Plains skink

This lizard is unusual in that it guards its eggs carefully while they incubate. The female helps the young wriggle free of their shells, and cares for them for about 10 days.

FOUND IN:
United States and Mexico

SIZE:
6-14 in

SCIENTIFIC NAME:
Eumeces obsoletus

Transvaal snake lizard

FOUND IN:
South Africa

SIZE:
16 in

SCIENTIFIC NAME:
Chamaesaura aena

With snakelike movements of its long body and tail, this lizard streaks through the grass in search of insects.

South African rain frog

The plump rain frog spends much of its life in underground burrows. It comes above ground only when it is raining to hunt insects and other small creatures.

FOUND IN:
South Africa

SIZE:
1¼ in

SCIENTIFIC NAME:
Breviceps adspersus

Boomslang

The tree-living boomslang is an extremely poisonous snake. It normally uses its venomous bite on lizards, frogs, and birds but can even kill humans.

FOUND IN:
Central to South Africa

SIZE:
up to 6½ ft

SCIENTIFIC NAME:
Dispholidus typus

Jungle runner

FOUND IN:
Central and South America

SIZE:
6-8 in

SCIENTIFIC NAME:
Ameiva ameiva

The jungle runner hunts on the ground and is an extremely active lizard. It has a long forked tongue, which it flicks out to search for insects and other small creatures.

Gopher snake

This large snake is a constrictor. It coils its body around its victim and squeezes until the prey suffocates. Mice, rats, birds, and lizards are its main prey.

FOUND IN:
Southwest Canada and United States

SIZE:
4-8 ft

SCIENTIFIC NAME:
Pituophis melanoleucas

Termite frog

As its name suggests, termites and ants are the main food of this frog. It climbs trees or digs into burrows to find the insects.

FOUND IN:
Africa, south of the Sahara

SIZE:
2 in

SCIENTIFIC NAME:
Phrynomerus bifasciatus

Tiger salamander

The large, brightly colored tiger salamander always lives near water, where it mates and lays its eggs. It often hunts at night, especially after rain, and takes prey such as earthworms, insects, and mice.

FOUND IN:
Southern Canada, United States, Mexico

SIZE:
6-16 in

SCIENTIFIC NAME:
Ambystoma tigrinum

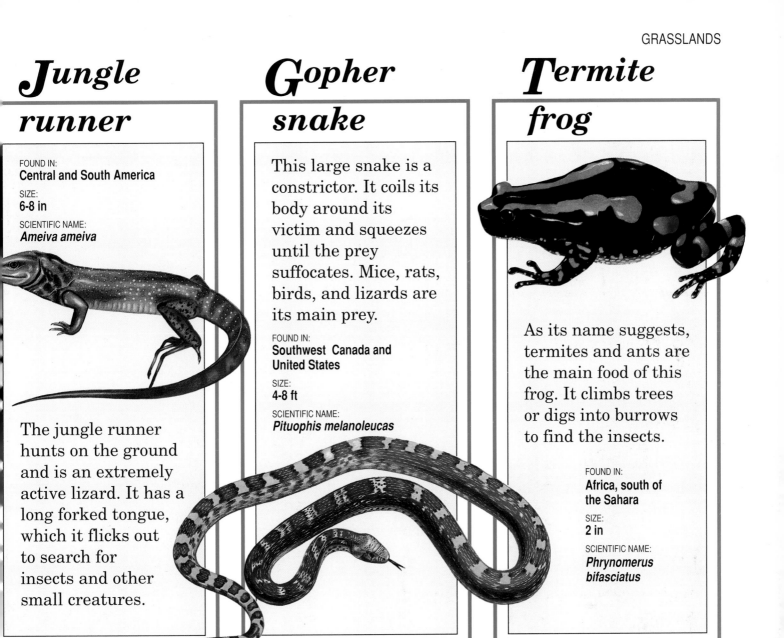

49

Deserts

The driest places in the world, where few plants can grow but a surprising number of animals manage to survive

Lack of water is what makes an area a desert. There is so little rain that the desert soil is dry, sandy, and mostly bare of plants. No rain means clear skies and few clouds so there is no shade from the sun. At midday the desert can become unbearably hot. But at night the heat goes away quickly and the air turns chilly. Tropical deserts are hot all year round in the daytime, but northern deserts, such as the Asian Gobi Desert, are cold in winter.

There are many different sorts of deserts. Some are full of sand dunes, others are covered with rocks and gravel. In some deserts the ground is smooth, bare stone; in others there are steep-sided hills and ravines.

No plants can grow in the driest areas, but most deserts have patches of damper soil, and nooks and crannies where tough plants can take root. In the semideserts that surround the true deserts there is a little more rain and more types of plants can grow.

Sagebrush and acacia are typical desert plants. They have small, pale, waxy leaves that can keep in moisture and will not scorch in the sun. Their long roots can reach as far as possible to find any water that is in the soil.

Some of the most famous desert plants, such as cacti and yuccas, have thick fleshy stems or leaves. When it does rain they absorb as much water as possible and store it in these. The biggest cactus can hold hundreds of pints of water to keep it alive through the dry months.

Other, short-lived, plants only appear after rainstorms. Their seeds lie buried in the sand for months or even years. When rain soaks the ground, they quickly sprout and burst into flower.

Only the toughest plants survive here in the middle of the Namib Desert in southwest Africa.

Life in the deserts

Deserts are difficult places for animals to live in but they are far from empty. They are home for lots of beetles, scorpions, lizards, snakes, and many other kinds of wildlife. All have ways of coping with the tough conditions.

Many of the smaller desert animals burrow underground to keep cool in the heat of the day. They come out to look for food when the sun sets, but go back to their burrows before the night becomes too cold.

Desert antelopes and other large animals try to find shade from the scorching sun beneath bushes or rocks.

Desert animals need water. Smaller creatures are usually able to get enough from the moisture in their food. Others, such as camels, may travel a long way to drink from scattered water holes and oases.

Food, like water, can also be

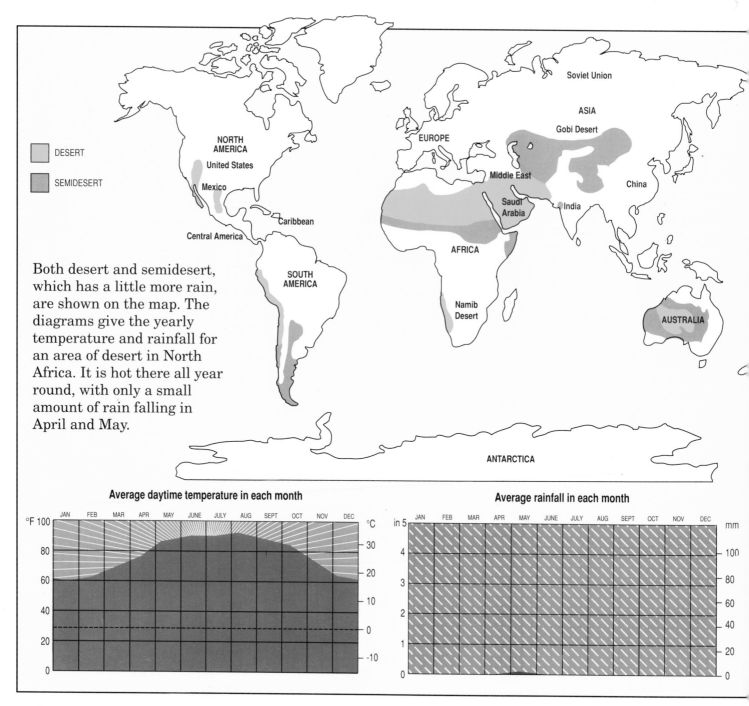

Both desert and semidesert, which has a little more rain, are shown on the map. The diagrams give the yearly temperature and rainfall for an area of desert in North Africa. It is hot there all year round, with only a small amount of rain falling in April and May.

DESERT

SEMIDESERT

Average daytime temperature in each month

Average rainfall in each month

hard to find. Gazelles, oryxes, and birds such as sandgrouse may roam over hundreds of miles of desert searching for a good meal.

Many animals make stores of food after heavy rainfall, when plants, seeds, and insects are more plentiful.

Cactus wren
UNITED STATES, MEXICO

To keep its eggs safe from predators, this wren makes its nest amid the sharp leaves of a yucca or on a prickly cactus.

Bactrian camel
ASIA

Body fat stored in the camel's humps helps keep it going when there is little food. Its thick fur protects the camel from the cold of the Gobi Desert winter.

Cream-colored courser
AFRICA, INDIA

Coursers run rather than fly and their coloring helps them stay hidden from enemies.

Thorny devil
AUSTRALIA

Few hunters would dare attack this Australian lizard. Protected by its spines, it searches for insects on the ground.

Fat-tailed gerbil
AFRICA

When food is plentiful, this gerbil's tail gets bigger. It holds a store of body fat to be used at times when food is scarce.

Fennec fox
AFRICA, MIDDLE EAST

Like many desert animals the fennec fox has large ears. These help it to lose excess heat from its body.

Pygmy rabbit

The pygmy rabbit stays in its burrow during the heat of the day. At night it comes out to feed on tough desert plants such as sagebrush.

FOUND IN:
United States

SIZE:
body 9-11 in; tail 1 in

SCIENTIFIC NAME:
Sylvilagus idahoensis

Pallas's cat

The long thick fur of Pallas's cat helps keep it warm during the cold winter of the Asian desert.

FOUND IN:
Central Asia

SIZE:
body 20-25 in; tail 8-12 in

SCIENTIFIC NAME:
Felis manul

Kowari

This small marsupial lives in an underground burrow. At night, it hunts for insects, lizards, and even small birds.

FOUND IN:
Central Australia

SIZE:
body 6-7 in; tail 5 in

SCIENTIFIC NAME:
Dasyuroides byrnei

Arabian oryx

The oryx is well designed for desert life. It can last long periods without water, getting the moisture it needs from its food. Using its horns and hooves, the oryx sometimes scrapes a hollow under a bush or sand dune in which to shelter from the sun.

FOUND IN:
Saudi Arabia

SIZE:
body 5 ft; tail 17 in

SCIENTIFIC NAME:
Oryx leucoryx

Red kangaroo

Like all marsupials, the red kangaroo has a pouch for its young. The newborn baby is less than an inch long but manages to clamber into the pouch. There it lives in safety for about eight months, feeding on its mother's milk.

FOUND IN:
Central Australia

SIZE:
body 3-5 ft; tail 35-40 in

SCIENTIFIC NAME:
Macropus rufus

Desert dormouse

The desert dormouse digs a burrow for shelter and may also hibernate there in winter. It catches insects but also stores seeds and other plant foods to eat during the winter months.

FOUND IN:
Soviet Union

SIZE:
body 2-3 in; tail 2-4 in

SCIENTIFIC NAME:
Selevinia betpakdalensis

Meerkat

FOUND IN:
Africa

SIZE:
body 9-12 in; tail 7-9 in

SCIENTIFIC NAME:
Suricata suricatta

Meerkats have very good eyesight and hearing. They often sit up on their hind legs to watch out for prey or for any sign of danger.

Desert hedgehog

Scorpions are a favorite food of this hedgehog; it nips off the stings before eating them. It also eats birds' eggs.

FOUND IN:
Northern Africa and Middle East

SIZE:
body 5-9 in; tail 1 in

SCIENTIFIC NAME:
Paraechinus aethiopicus

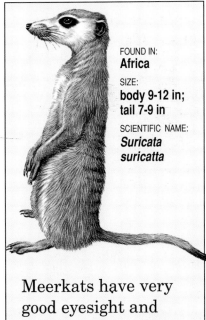

Focus on: The American Southwest

American deserts are famous for their cactus plants. Most of the world's 1,500 different types live here, including the giant saguaro cactus which may grow 50 feet high. These strange plants, which have swollen green stems full of water and few leaves, provide some food and shelter for desert wildlife.

Although they are covered with sharp thorns and spines, cactus plants are gnawed and eaten by pack rats and the piglike peccary. Various insects are attracted to the flowers and fruit, and Costa's hummingbird sips nectar from cactus flowers.

Cactus wrens nest among the spines, while woodpeckers drill nest holes in the swollen stems.

In some parts of the Southwest, heavy rain falls once or twice a year and brings the desert to life. Small, colorful flowers, such as desert marigolds and bluebonnets, sprout from

Verdin
This common desert bird makes its nest among the protective spines of a cactus.

Greater roadrunner
One of the fastest runners of all flying birds, the greater roadrunner can race along at up to 12 miles an hour.

Desert night lizard
At night this lizard clambers over yucca and agave plants in search of insects to eat.

Mourning dove
Seeds are the main food of this dove, but it also catches insects and snails.

Western blind snake
Its sense of smell guides this snake to ant and termite nests. It goes right into the nests to feed on the insects.

seeds that may have lain buried in the dry desert soil for months.

Insects hatch out to feed on flower nectar and pollen and on fresh leaves. Desert rodents busily collect seeds. This is also a good time for hunters such as lizards and birds to snap up prey such as wasps, flies, and beetles.

Desert cottontail
This rabbit is liveliest in the evening when it feeds on leaves, fruit, and any other plant food it can find.

Elf owl
A hole in a cactus plant makes an ideal nesting place for this tiny owl.

Gila monster
When food is scarce, this lizard can live off the body fat stored in its large tail.

Kangaroo rat
Well suited to desert life, this rodent can survive without ever drinking. It gets enough moisture from its food.

57

Red-tailed hawk

FOUND IN:
North and Central America, Caribbean

SIZE:
20-25 in

SCIENTIFIC NAME:
Buteo jamaicensis

A powerful, aggressive bird, this hawk can live anywhere from forest to desert. It hunts other birds in the air or swoops down on rabbits and lizards from a high perch. It makes its nest on the branch of a tree or cactus.

Cinnamon quail-thrush

After sheltering from the heat of the day in a hole or burrow, this bird comes out at dusk to feed on seeds and insects.

FOUND IN:
Australia

SIZE:
8 in

SCIENTIFIC NAME:
Cinclosoma cinnamomeum

Pallas's sandgrouse

The male of this bird has special absorbent feathers on his belly. He uses these to carry water to his young.

FOUND IN:
Soviet Union and China

SIZE:
12-16 in

SCIENTIFIC NAME:
Syrrhaptes paradoxus

Desert lark

According to the color of the sand where they live, desert larks have darker or lighter plumage which camouflages them from their enemies.

FOUND IN:
Africa and Middle East

SIZE:
6 in

SCIENTIFIC NAME:
Ammomanes deserti

Vermilion flycatcher

FOUND IN:
Southern United States, Central America, South America

SIZE:
5-7 in

SCIENTIFIC NAME:
Pyrocephalus rubinus

This flycatcher darts out from a high perch to catch bees and other flying insects.

Zebra finch

FOUND IN:
Australia

SIZE:
4 in

SCIENTIFIC NAME:
Poephila guttata

The zebra finch usually breeds after heavy rainfall when there is plenty of food. It makes its nest in a low bush or tree.

Karroo scrub-robin

The lively scrub-robin spends much of its time on the ground, where it searches for insects and seeds to eat.

FOUND IN:
Africa

SIZE:
6 in

SCIENTIFIC NAME:
Erythropygia coryphaeus

Lappet-faced vulture

Like all vultures, this bird is a scavenger—it feeds on the bodies of dead animals. Its head is bare so it can plunge deep inside a carcass without dirtying any of its feathers. The lappet-faced is the most powerful of all the African vultures.

FOUND IN:
Africa

SIZE:
39-41 in

SCIENTIFIC NAME:
Aegypius tracheliotus

59

Saw-scaled adder

An extremely dangerous snake, this adder has a poisonous bite that can kill a human. Usually, however, it hunts mice, frogs, and lizards.

FOUND IN:
Northern Africa, Middle East, India

SIZE:
20-28 in

SCIENTIFIC NAME:
Echis carinatus

Sandfish

Using its strong legs and toes, this lizard pushes itself along as though it is swimming through the sand. It feeds on beetles and other insects.

FOUND IN:
Saudi Arabia

SIZE:
up to 8 in

SCIENTIFIC NAME:
Scincus philbyi

Arabian toad-headed agamid

A burrowing lizard, this agamid digs tunnels for shelter or buries itself in the sand. If alarmed, it takes up a defensive position to warn off the enemy—it lifts its tail high, rolls it up, and unrolls it again.

FOUND IN:
Middle East

SIZE:
up to 5 in

SCIENTIFIC NAME:
Phrynocephalus nejdensis

Chuckwalla

FOUND IN:
Southern United States and Mexico

SIZE:
11-16 in

SCIENTIFIC NAME:
Sauromalus obesus

Folds of skin at the chuckwalla's sides contain special glands in which it can store liquid. It makes use of this in dry seasons.

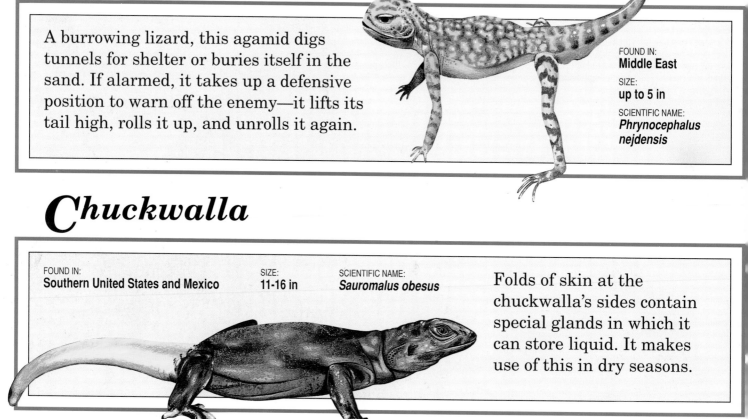

Western blue-tongued skink

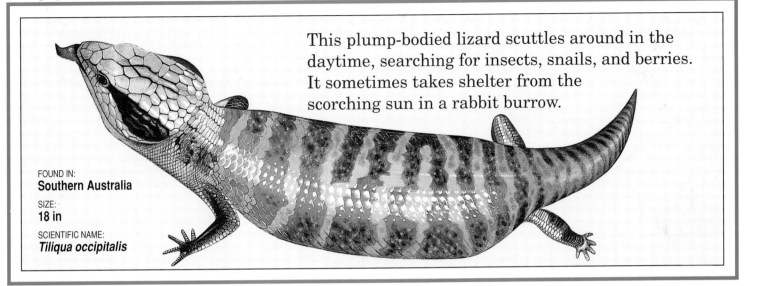

This plump-bodied lizard scuttles around in the daytime, searching for insects, snails, and berries. It sometimes takes shelter from the scorching sun in a rabbit burrow.

FOUND IN:
Southern Australia

SIZE:
18 in

SCIENTIFIC NAME:
Tiliqua occipitalis

Web-footed gecko

Rain is almost unknown where this gecko lives. It laps dew from the stones and even licks its own eyes for moisture.

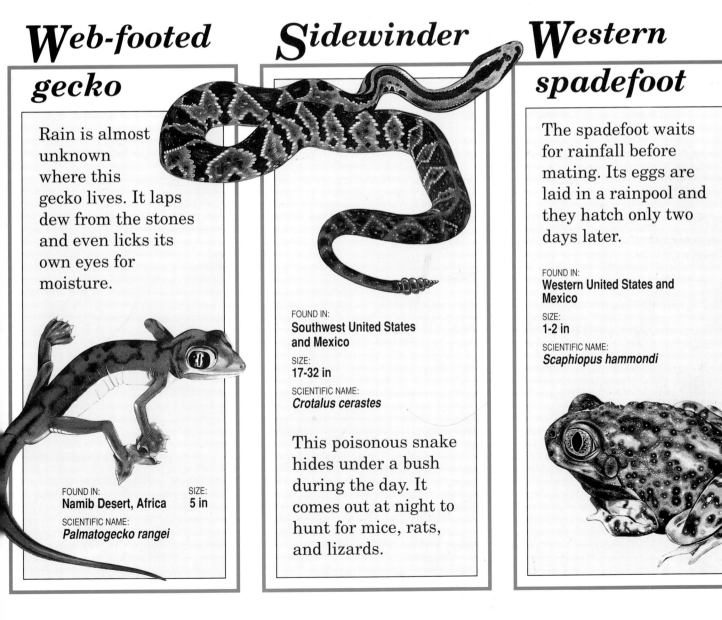

FOUND IN:
Namib Desert, Africa

SIZE:
5 in

SCIENTIFIC NAME:
Palmatogecko rangei

Sidewinder

FOUND IN:
Southwest United States and Mexico

SIZE:
17-32 in

SCIENTIFIC NAME:
Crotalus cerastes

This poisonous snake hides under a bush during the day. It comes out at night to hunt for mice, rats, and lizards.

Western spadefoot

The spadefoot waits for rainfall before mating. Its eggs are laid in a rainpool and they hatch only two days later.

FOUND IN:
Western United States and Mexico

SIZE:
1-2 in

SCIENTIFIC NAME:
Scaphiopus hammondi

Tropical forests

Home to a huge variety of the most spectacular insects, frogs, snakes, birds, and monkeys

The thick forests that grow in the tropics are teeming with life. Nobody knows exactly how many plants and animals there are living among these dense groups of trees, but there may be nearly as many kinds as in all the other habitats put together.

Some of these forests are extremely hot and have heavy rainfall all year round. These are known as tropical rainforests. There are many different kinds of trees in the rainforests but most have a similar shape. Their trunks rise straight up from the forest floor for 50 to 65 feet before branching out and growing leaves. Together their leaves cluster into a thick, green roof, or canopy, over the forest, about 100 feet from the ground. A few, even taller, trees tower above the canopy. Underneath, in the shade, stand smaller trees, palms, and giant ferns.

Rainforest trees often have other plants living on them. Vines and creepers trail from the treetops to the ground. Plants such as orchids squat on branches, dangling their roots so that they can soak up moisture straight from the damp air.

In other parts of the tropics there are forests which have heavy rain for only part of the year. For this reason they are called seasonal forests. The plant life is less dense than in the rainforests, and the trees may lose their leaves in the dry season.

The forest floor also looks different from one type of forest to another. In seasonal forests, where the canopy makes less shade, there may be plenty of small bushes and undergrowth. But deep inside the rainforests, so little light manages to get through the dense canopy that the floor is dark and quite bare.

Two gorillas emerge from the dense mountain rainforest in the west of Africa.

Life in the tropical forests

High in the canopy is one of the best places in the forest for animals to live. There is plenty of shelter, and leaves, fruit, and flowers on which to feed. Not only do flying animals such as birds, bats, and butterflies live up here, there are also crabs, frogs, lizards, and just about any animal that can climb. Some, such as monkeys and squirrels, rarely leave the treetops and simply leap from branch to branch.

Other animals prefer to live lower down in the layer of smaller trees. Many of these, such as lemurs, are not really climbing animals and spend much of their time on the forest floor. Forest kingfishers and other birds perch a few feet off the ground ready to pounce on their prey.

Big, hoofed animals, such as antelopes, pigs, and deer, cannot climb at all. They wander over the shady floor

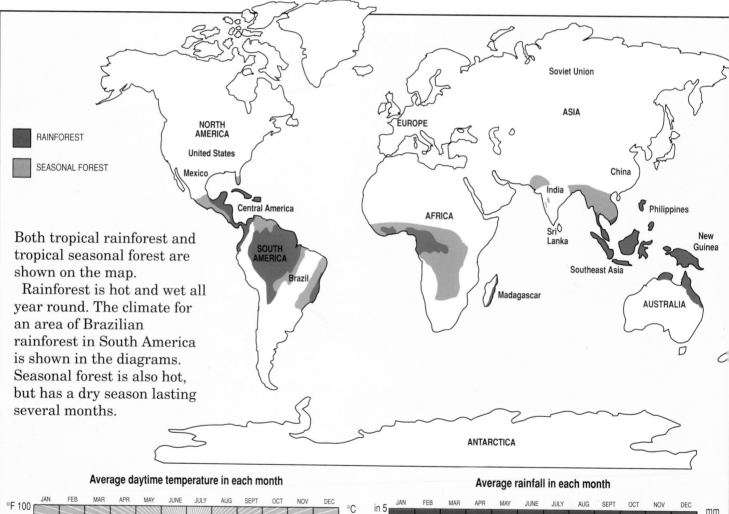

RAINFOREST

SEASONAL FOREST

Soviet Union

ASIA

NORTH AMERICA

EUROPE

United States

Mexico

China

India

Central America

AFRICA

Philippines

SOUTH AMERICA

Sri Lanka

New Guinea

Brazil

Southeast Asia

Madagascar

AUSTRALIA

ANTARCTICA

Both tropical rainforest and tropical seasonal forest are shown on the map.

Rainforest is hot and wet all year round. The climate for an area of Brazilian rainforest in South America is shown in the diagrams. Seasonal forest is also hot, but has a dry season lasting several months.

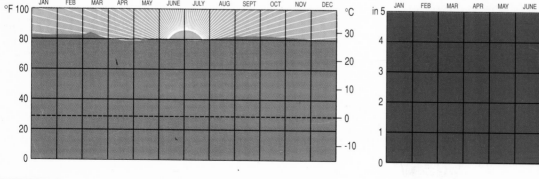

Average daytime temperature in each month

°F 100

80

60

40

20

0

°C

30

20

10

0

-10

JAN FEB MAR APR MAY JUNE JULY AUG SEPT OCT NOV DEC

Average rainfall in each month

in 5

4

3

2

1

0

mm

100

80

60

40

20

0

JAN FEB MAR APR MAY JUNE JULY AUG SEPT OCT NOV DEC

nibbling bushes and rummaging for leaves, fruit, nuts, and seeds that have dropped from the trees.

Any fallen food does not last long. If it is not eaten whole, there are armies of worms, beetles, ants, and other creatures living in the soil that chew it to bits.

Blue bird of paradise

NEW GUINEA

The male bird uses his beautiful feathers in a display to attract a mate.

Emerald tree boa

SOUTH AMERICA

This brightly colored snake can cling to branches with its muscular tail while it watches for prey.

Scarlet macaw

MEXICO, CENTRAL AMERICA, SOUTH AMERICA

This macaw thrives in the rainforest where it can find a variety of seeds and fruits.

Great Indian hornbill

INDIA, SOUTHEAST ASIA

Using its long beak, the hornbill can reach out for fruits and berries at the ends of branches.

Okapi

AFRICA

The long tongue of the okapi helps it reach leaves and buds on forest trees.

Orangutan

SOUTHEAST ASIA

Using its long, powerful arms, the orangutan can climb to all levels of the trees in search of food.

65

Lar gibbon

FOUND IN:
Southeast Asia

SIZE:
16-23 in

SCIENTIFIC NAME:
Hylobates lar

This ape swings through the trees on its long arms or runs upright along the branches. It feeds mainly on fruit, leaves, shoots, buds, and flowers, but occasionally eats insects.

Tube-nosed fruit bat

Using its sharp teeth, this bat chews ripe fruit to extract the juice. It drops the pulp to the ground.

FOUND IN:
Southeast Asia, New Guinea, Australia

SIZE:
body 3-5 in; tail up to 1 in

SCIENTIFIC NAME:
Nyctimene major

Two-toed sloth

The sloth rarely comes to the ground. It eats, sleeps, and even gives birth hanging in the trees.

FOUND IN:
Northern South America

SIZE:
23-25 in

SCIENTIFIC NAME:
Choloepus didactylus

Gorilla

The gorilla can climb but spends most of its life on the ground where it normally walks on all fours. It is a gentle, peaceful creature and feeds mainly on leaves, buds, berries, and bark.

FOUND IN:
Africa

SIZE:
male 5-6 ft; female 4-5 ft

SCIENTIFIC NAME:
Gorilla gorilla

Slender loris

FOUND IN:
Sri Lanka and southern India

SIZE:
7-10 in

SCIENTIFIC NAME:
Loris tardigradus

The slender loris spends most of its life in trees where it moves slowly and carefully on its long, thin legs. It eats insects, lizards, birds, and eggs.

Philippine flying lemur

The flying lemur flies with the help of flaps of skin at its sides. With legs and flaps outstretched, the lemur can glide up to 450 feet between trees. It feeds on fruit, buds, and flowers.

FOUND IN:
Philippines

SIZE:
body 15-17 in; tail 8-10 in

SCIENTIFIC NAME:
Cynocephalus volans

Red howler

The male howler monkey has an extremely loud call. Its shouts can be heard from nearly 2 miles away.

FOUND IN:
South America

SIZE:
body 31-36 in; tail 31-36 in

SCIENTIFIC NAME:
Alouatta seniculus

Golden lion tamarin

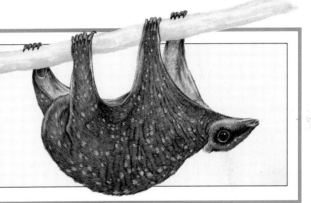

The beautiful tamarin has a silky golden mane that covers its head and shoulders and hides its ears. A nimble little creature, it leaps from branch to branch searching for insects, lizards, and small birds to eat.

FOUND IN:
Southeast Brazil

SIZE:
body 7-9 in; tail 10-13 in

SCIENTIFIC NAME:
Leontopithecus rosalia

Focus on: *The Amazon rainforest*

The South American rainforest is the largest in the world. The area is known as Amazonia, after the River Amazon which flows through the forest.

Some extraordinary animals live in the Amazon forest. There are spiders large enough to catch birds, giant snakes, and huge colonies of ants that march across the forest floor devouring any small animal in their path.

But the forest wildlife is not always easy to see. Some animals only come out at night; others hide in the darkness of the forest floor. Tapirs and the piglike peccaries—mammals that nose through the ground layer for any fallen food—quickly dash away into the gloom.

Other animals live high in the trees. Giant butterflies and tiny hummingbirds sip nectar from flowers. Gaudy toucans and parrots pluck fruit and nuts from branches. There are also many kinds of monkeys living in the trees, including the pygmy marmoset which can sit in a human hand.

In the last 80 years much of this wonderful forest has been destroyed by logging, mining, and ranching. If the damage is not stopped soon, there will be no rainforest left in the next century.

Yellow-headed parrot
Small groups of these parrots feed in the treetops on fruit, seeds, nuts, and berries.

Black spider monkey
This acrobatic monkey uses its long tail as an extra limb to hold onto branches as it moves through the trees.

Ocelot
At night this stealthy hunter comes out of its daytime hiding place to prey on deer, birds, and other small animals.

Brazilian tapir
Although a land animal, the tapir is a good swimmer and diver. It feeds on leaves, fruits, and water plants.

68

Harpy eagle
An extremely fierce and powerful bird, the harpy can kill animals as large as monkeys and sloths.

Tamandua
This anteater breaks into ant and termite nests with its strong claws and feeds on the insects.

Amazonian umbrellabird
The extraordinary umbrellabird springs noisily through the trees, searching for fruit and insects.

Snail-eating snake
This snake feeds entirely on snails. It pushes its long jaw into the shell, sinks its teeth into the snail's soft body, and pulls it out.

Horned frog
Snails, smaller frogs, and mice are all eaten by this large plump frog, which lives on the forest floor.

69

Coati

FOUND IN:
South America

SIZE:
body 17-26 in; tail 17-26 in

SCIENTIFIC NAME:
Nasua nasua

With its long nose, the coati probes into holes and cracks in the ground, searching for insects, spiders, and small animals to eat.

Indian striped squirrel

FOUND IN:
India and Sri Lanka

SIZE:
body 4-7 in; tail 4-7 in

SCIENTIFIC NAME:
Funambulus palmarum

This squirrel lives in palm forest and feeds on the nuts, flowers, and buds of the palm.

Bamboo rat

Using its sharp teeth and claws, this rat digs down under clumps of bamboo to feed on the roots.

FOUND IN:
Southeast Asia

SIZE:
body 14-19 in; tail 4-6 in

SCIENTIFIC NAME:
Rhizomys sumatrensis

Indian elephant

The Indian elephant has smaller ears than the African elephant and a more humped back. It feeds on leaves and grass, which it picks with its long trunk.

FOUND IN:
India, Sri Lanka, Southeast Asia

SIZE:
body 18-21 ft; tail 4-5 ft

SCIENTIFIC NAME:
Elephas maximus

Tiger

The mighty tiger
is the largest and
most powerful of
the big cats.
It usually lives
alone and hunts deer
and other animals at
night. Tigers are now
rare and most live
on reserves
in India.

FOUND IN:
**Soviet Union,
China, India,
Southeast Asia**

SIZE:
**body 6-9 ft;
tail 3 ft**

SCIENTIFIC NAME:
Panthera tigris

Bongo

FOUND IN:
Africa

SIZE:
body 5-8 ft; tail 17-25 in

SCIENTIFIC NAME:
Tragelaphus euryceros

The shy bongo hides among
bushes and trees in the day.
At dawn and dusk it comes out
to feed on leaves, bark, and fruit.

Bearded pig

FOUND IN:
Southeast Asia

SIZE:
body 5-6 ft; tail 7-12 in

SCIENTIFIC NAME:
Sus barbatus

Fallen fruit, roots,
and insect young are
the main foods of this
pig. It often follows
monkeys to pick up
the fruit they drop as
they feed.

Jaguar

The jaguar often
climbs trees, where
it lies in wait for prey.
It is also a good
swimmer and feeds on fish and
turtles as well as on deer and other mammals.

FOUND IN:
**Southwest United States,
Central America, South America**

SIZE:
**body 5-6 ft;
tail 27-36 in**

SCIENTIFIC NAME:
Panthera onca

71

King vulture

FOUND IN:
Mexico, Central America, South America

SIZE:
30 in

SCIENTIFIC NAME:
Sarcoramphus papa

The bare skin on this vulture's head is marked with gaudy patterns, making it a very colorful bird. It feeds mostly on carrion—the bodies of dead animals—but it also eats dying fish that it finds stranded on riverbanks.

Indian peafowl

In the wild, the peafowl lives in dense forest where it feeds on berries, green plants, insects, and other small animals. Only the male has the spectacular tail feathers.

FOUND IN:
India and Sri Lanka

SIZE:
male (with tail) 6-7 ft; female 34 in

SCIENTIFIC NAME:
Pavo cristatus

Frilled coquette

With the help of its long, curved bill, this bird sucks nectar from flowers. It also eats fruit and insects.

FOUND IN:
Brazil

SIZE:
3 in

SCIENTIFIC NAME:
Lophornis magnifica

Purple honeycreeper

The honeycreeper eats fruit and insects but also sucks nectar from flowers, using its long, curved bill.

FOUND IN:
Trinidad and South America

SIZE:
4 in

SCIENTIFIC NAME:
Cyanerpes caeruleus

Eclectus parrot

FOUND IN:
New Guinea and northeast Australia

SIZE:
15-18 in

SCIENTIFIC NAME:
Eclectus roratus

The male eclectus parrot has mostly green feathers, while the female is bright red with a blue belly. Both feed mainly on fruit, nuts, flowers, and nectar.

Female   Male

Beautiful paradise kingfisher

FOUND IN:
New Guinea and Moluccas

SIZE:
13-17 in

SCIENTIFIC NAME:
Tanysiptera galatea

Perched low on a branch, this kingfisher watches for prey such as insects and lizards. It also digs for earthworms in the forest soil.

At nesting time, a pair digs a hole in a termite nest in a tree where the female lays her eggs.

African emerald cuckoo

Like many cuckoos, this one lays her eggs in the nests of other birds such as bulbuls and orioles. When the cuckoo chick hatches, it usually throws any other eggs or young out of the nest.

FOUND IN:
Africa, south of the Sahara

SIZE:
8 in

SCIENTIFIC NAME:
Chrysococcyx cupreus

Spot-billed toucanet

Berries and fruits are the main foods of this toucanet. It swallows them whole and then regurgitates and spits out the skins and stones. In this way the birds help spread the seeds of plants through the forest.

FOUND IN:
South America

SIZE:
13 in

SCIENTIFIC NAME:
Selenidera maculirostris

Leaf-tailed gecko

The spotted pattern on the body of this gecko blends well with tree bark and helps keep it hidden as it lies pressed against a tree trunk. It feeds mainly on insects.

FOUND IN:
Madagascar

SIZE:
8 in

SCIENTIFIC NAME:
Uroplatus fimbriatus

Golden arrow-poison frog

The brilliant colors of this frog warn enemies that its skin contains poisonous substances. The poison is used by tribesmen on the tips of arrows.

FOUND IN:
Central and South America

SIZE:
1-2 in

SCIENTIFIC NAME:
Dendrobates auratus

Boa constrictor

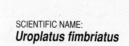

The boa constrictor kills its prey by wrapping the victim in the strong coils of its body until it is suffocated or crushed to death.

SIZE:
up to 18 ft

SCIENTIFIC NAME:
Constrictor constrictor

FOUND IN:
Mexico, Central America, South America

Paradise tree snake

This snake is an excellent climber and spends much of its life in trees. Also known as the flying snake, it can launch itself into the air and glide from tree to tree in the forest.

FOUND IN:
Southeast Asia

SIZE:
up to 4 ft

SCIENTIFIC NAME:
Chrysopelea paradisi

Common iguana

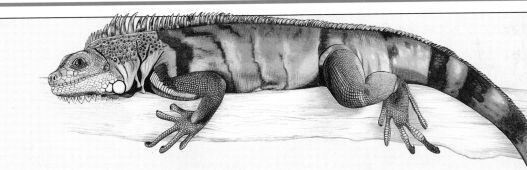

FOUND IN:
**Northern and central
South America;
introduced in United States**

SIZE:
up to 6 ft

SCIENTIFIC NAME:
Iguana iguana

An active, tree-living lizard, the iguana also swims well. It has sharp teeth and claws and defends itself fiercely when attacked. It feeds mainly on plants.

Wallace's flying frog

FOUND IN:
Southeast Asia

SIZE:
4 in

SCIENTIFIC NAME:
Rhacophorus nigropalmatus

This frog does not fly but glides from tree to tree. Webbed feet and flaps of skin on its legs act like a parachute to help it float through the air.

Marsupial frog

The marsupial frog has an unusual way of caring for its eggs. The female carries them in a special pouch on her back until they are ready to hatch.

FOUND IN:
South America

SIZE:
1-2 in

SCIENTIFIC NAME:
Gastrotheca marsupiata

Schweigger's hingeback tortoise

This tortoise feeds mainly on plants but also eats some small animals. It has a unique shell. A hinge allows the rear of the shell to be lowered to protect the animal's hindquarters if it is attacked.

FOUND IN:
West and Central Africa

SIZE:
13 in

SCIENTIFIC NAME:
Kinixys erosa

Mountains

Howling winds, steep slopes, and bare rocks make the tops of high mountains harsh and lonely places

Anyone who has climbed a mountain knows that it is much colder at the top than in the valleys far below. On average, the air temperature falls about one degree Fahrenheit with every 300 feet.

It is often warm enough on the lower slopes of mountains for trees to grow, but at a certain height it becomes too cold. The height at which trees stop growing is known as the treeline and varies from place to place, depending on the climate. Above this, the slopes are much more open, with meadows of grass and mountain flowers between the rocks and crags. On top of the highest peaks there may be a cap of ice and snow all year round. The height at which this begins is the snowline.

Only certain types of plants can grow high above the treeline because of the cold, windy, and steep conditions. Many of these plants are small, with a compact bushy shape that helps keep them warm and out of the wind. Others, such as the alpine lily, have very flexible stems that can bend in the wind without snapping. The famous edelweiss is one of many mountain plants with leaves that are covered in furry hairs to keep them warm at night. Plants also make their own warmth—the alpine soldanella produces enough heat to melt a hole in snow.

The soil is thin on mountain slopes, so plants must have plenty of roots to help them find enough water and to anchor them against the gales. It is too cold for plants to grow quickly and most take several years to flower.

Above the snowline, there is very little plant food for animals—just a few lichens and mosses clinging to the rocks, and special algae that live on the ice. These algae contain a kind of antifreeze substance that keeps their sap from freezing and killing the plant.

Sure-footed Dall sheep perch on a narrow ledge high on Mount McKinley in Alaska.

Life in the mountains

Mountain animals grow thick fur to keep out the cold. Some even have double-layered coats. Many rodents burrow into the soil to keep warm and out of the wind at night, and small birds huddle in crevices, sharing one another's body heat.

The weather becomes even worse in winter. Snow falls and some of it slides and tumbles downhill in avalanches. At this time most animals move down from the high slopes or hide underground. But there are some that remain, pushing the snow aside to reach their food. The ibex, a type of goat, often keeps to steep cliffs, where snow does not settle.

Strong gales make flying difficult. Small birds fly low over the ground to avoid being swept downwind. Big, strong-winged birds, such as condors and eagles, manage better and use the winds to help their soaring flight.

Most mountains are made when rocks are pushed upward by movements of the Earth's crust.

The main mountain ranges in the world are shown on the map. The heights of the tallest peaks in each continent are given below. These peaks are marked on the map by red triangles.

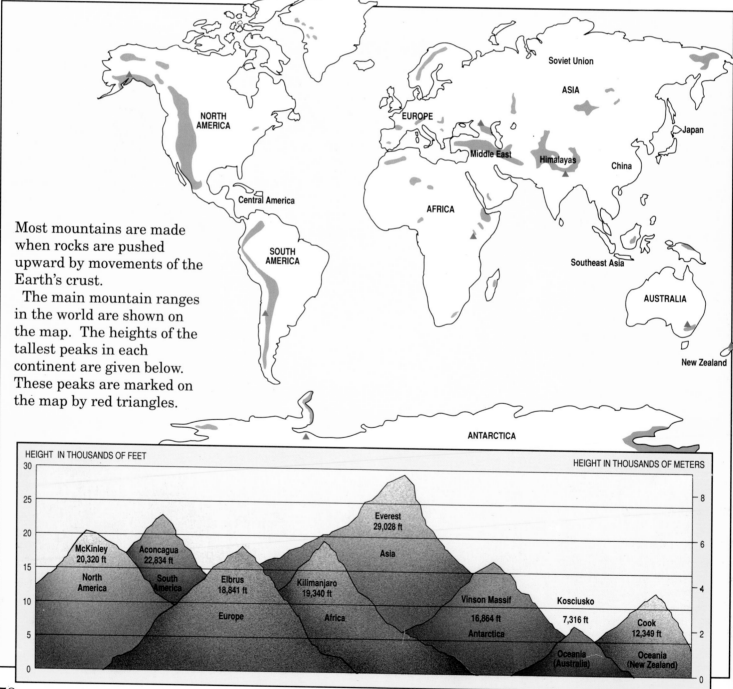

Animals need a firm foothold on steep, rocky slopes. Mountain goats and sheep have special pads on their hooves that grip the rocks in the same way that a car tire grips the road. Other animals have claws and stiff hairs on their feet to stop them slipping.

Golden eagle
NORTH AMERICA, EUROPE, NORTHERN ASIA
This magnificent bird can soar high over the mountain slopes searching for prey. If it spots something, it dives down to seize it in its talons.

Snow finch
EUROPE, ASIA
At night the snow finch often takes shelter in the burrow of a rodent or other mammal.

Andean condor
SOUTH AMERICA
Soaring for hours on its huge outstretched wings, the condor is strong enough to survive the fiercest winds.

Mountain goat
NORTH AMERICA
The sure-footed mountain goat has a long, hairy coat and thick underfur to keep it warm.

Chinchilla-rat
SOUTH AMERICA
Small groups of these creatures live in rock crevices high in the mountains, feeding on any plants they can find.

79

Chamois

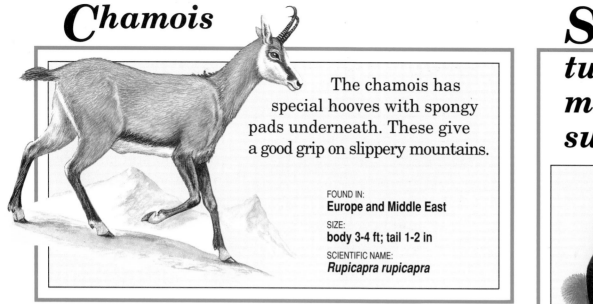

The chamois has special hooves with spongy pads underneath. These give a good grip on slippery mountains.

FOUND IN:
Europe and Middle East

SIZE:
body 3-4 ft; tail 1-2 in

SCIENTIFIC NAME:
Rupicapra rupicapra

Peregrine falcon

When hunting, the peregrine makes a fast dive at its prey, often a pigeon or dove, and kills it with its strong talons.

FOUND IN:
almost worldwide

SIZE:
15-20 in

SCIENTIFIC NAME:
Falco peregrinus

Vicuna

The vicuna is an agile animal which can move at up to 30 miles an hour, even on steep slopes. It feeds on grass and other small plants.

FOUND IN:
South America

SIZE:
body 4-5 ft; tail 6 in

SCIENTIFIC NAME:
Vicugna vicugna

Scarlet-tufted malachite sunbird

FOUND IN:
Africa

SIZE:
male 10-12 in; female 5-6 in

SCIENTIFIC NAME:
Nectarinia johnstoni

This sunbird lives only on high mountain slopes, where it feeds on the nectar of giant lobelias and protea flowers. It also eats many insects. Both male and female have scarlet tufts, but only the male has long tail feathers.

Andean solitaire

FOUND IN:
Central and South America

SIZE:
7 in

SCIENTIFIC NAME:
Myadestes ralloides

The solitaire lives in the Andes Mountains at heights of up to 15,000 feet. It has a pure, clear voice and sings all year round.

Temminck's tragopan

The favorite home of this beautiful bird is cool, damp mountain forest. It eats leaves, berries, and insects. The female bird has light-brown feathers.

FOUND IN:
China and Southeast Asia

SIZE:
25 in

SCIENTIFIC NAME:
Tragopan temminckii

Northern pika

In summer, the pika makes little piles of grass and stems. In winter it tunnels through the snow to reach its food stores.

FOUND IN:
Soviet Union, China, Japan, North America

SIZE:
8-10 in

SCIENTIFIC NAME:
Ochotona alpina

Mountain lion

Deer are the main prey of this hunter. Having stalked its victim, the mountain lion pounces and kills with a swift bite to the neck.

FOUND IN:
North America, Central America, South America

SIZE:
body 3-5 ft; tail 23-33 in

SCIENTIFIC NAME:
Felis concolor

Focus on: *The Himalayas*

The tallest peaks in the world are found in the Himalayas, a range of mountains to the north of India. Temperatures there fall well below freezing, the gales are furious, and deep snow reaches far downhill.

On the lower slopes of the Himalayas are thick forests where animals such as brightly colored pheasants and red pandas make their homes. But higher up, where the trees stop and there are just rocks, grass, and scattered bushes, animals find life much harder.

Herds of wild goats and sheep roam across grassy slopes, looking for small plants to nibble. Most move down to the forests in winter when the weather is at its worst. Such a journey would be too far and too dangerous for small rodents. Some, such as the Himalayan marmot, hibernate instead, but the Asian pika remains awake through the winter. It lives on the grass and leaves it has stored among rocks.

In winter, when food is harder to find, small birds fly to warmer areas. But the big birds of prey, such as the golden eagle and the lammergeier, remain. They can soar for hours on their large wings, scanning whole valleys for food.

Himalayan snowcock
The gray and white plumage of the snowcock blends well with the rocks and snows of its mountain home.

Ibisbill
Using its long beak, the ibisbill probes in stony riverbeds for small fish to eat.

Tahr
The goatlike tahr climbs and leaps around the mountainside with ease. It lives in herds and feeds on almost any plants it can reach.

Lammergeier
Like other vultures, this bird feeds on dead animals.

Yak
A coat of long hair, reaching almost to the ground, protects the yak from the Himalayan cold.

Wallcreeper
In its search for insects to feed on, this bird climbs up cliff faces, searching every crevice.

83

Rivers and lakes

A spectacular range of animals live in the rivers and lakes of the world, from tiny insects to giant fishes and crocodiles

When rain falls on hilly land, it soaks into the soil and runs in trickles down slopes and into hollows in the ground. Water always flows downhill if it can, so it soon runs into a valley stream or river. As the river keeps going downhill, it joins with neighboring streams and rivers and becomes bigger and bigger. Eventually the river flows into the sea.

The water in streams and rivers is called fresh water because it is almost pure, not salty like the sea. Compared with the vast oceans, there is very little fresh water on Earth, but there is enough to make countless rivers of all sizes. Where fresh water collects in hollows and on flat plains, ponds, lakes, marshes, and swamps form.

Rivers and lakes appear in many different areas and climates so the plants and animals that live in them vary from place to place. Some mountain streams and lakes are so cold and clear that there does not seem to be much life in them at all. But many lowland ponds and rivers seem to be choked with plant life. Usually, the more plants there are in a freshwater habitat, the more kinds of animals are found there.

Reeds, irises, rushes, and other plants with stems that rise above the water grow in shallow water, along the riverbanks and in marshes. Even certain trees grow in swampy, waterlogged soil.

Other plants grow under water, usually in places where the bottom is muddy rather than stony. They do not need stiff stems like land plants because the water holds them upright. Instead their stems are flexible so that they can bend without snapping.

A burly Alaskan brown bear plunges into a fast-flowing river in search of fish to eat.

Life in rivers and lakes

Some animals, such as otters and kingfishers, only go into the water to find food. But most freshwater animals live in water all the time.

Fish are the best equipped for life in rivers and lakes. They use their fins and tails to push themselves through the water. Many kinds of fishes, particularly those in deep lakes, spend all their time out in the open water, but others live on the bottom, rummaging for food in the mud. Leeches and the young of some insects attach themselves to stones on the river bottom. This stops them from being swept away in the strong current.

Water beetles and snails are some of the animals that live among water plants. Leaves floating on the surface make useful platforms for animals to sit on. Frogs rest on large lily pads, and dragonflies often land on leaves.

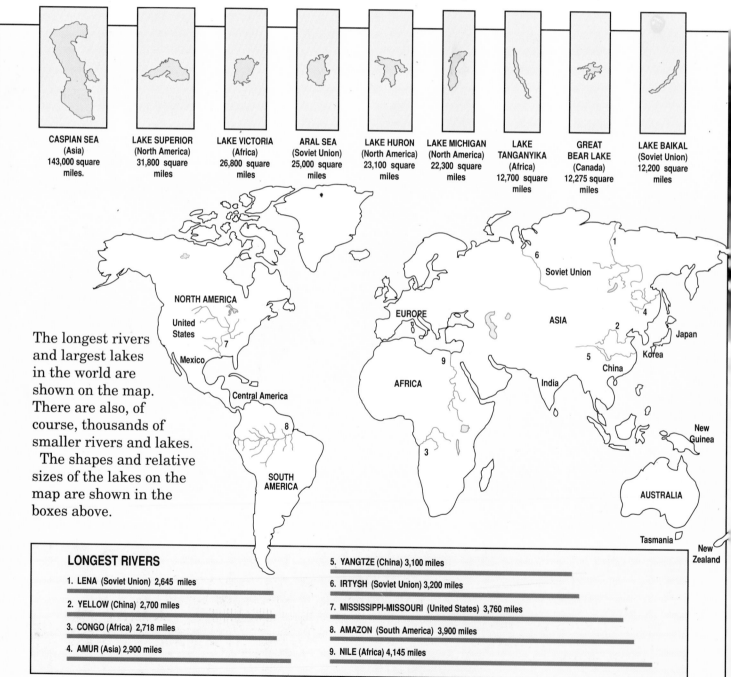

| CASPIAN SEA (Asia) 143,000 square miles. | LAKE SUPERIOR (North America) 31,800 square miles | LAKE VICTORIA (Africa) 26,800 square miles | ARAL SEA (Soviet Union) 25,000 square miles | LAKE HURON (North America) 23,100 square miles | LAKE MICHIGAN (North America) 22,300 square miles | LAKE TANGANYIKA (Africa) 12,700 square miles | GREAT BEAR LAKE (Canada) 12,275 square miles | LAKE BAIKAL (Soviet Union) 12,200 square miles |

The longest rivers and largest lakes in the world are shown on the map. There are also, of course, thousands of smaller rivers and lakes.

The shapes and relative sizes of the lakes on the map are shown in the boxes above.

LONGEST RIVERS

1. LENA (Soviet Union) 2,645 miles
2. YELLOW (China) 2,700 miles
3. CONGO (Africa) 2,718 miles
4. AMUR (Asia) 2,900 miles
5. YANGTZE (China) 3,100 miles
6. IRTYSH (Soviet Union) 3,200 miles
7. MISSISSIPPI-MISSOURI (United States) 3,760 miles
8. AMAZON (South America) 3,900 miles
9. NILE (Africa) 4,145 miles

Plants that grow up out of the water are home for lots of creatures. Many, such as the tiny harvest mouse which climbs up reed stems and the birds that roost among reeds at night, live above the water because it is harder for their enemies to reach them there.

Gray heron
EUROPE, ASIA, AFRICA
By stretching out its long neck, the heron can fish from the riverbank. It seizes prey in its daggerlike bill.

Anaconda
SOUTH AMERICA
This snake can stay underwater for up to 10 minutes as it lies in wait for prey.

Giant otter
SOUTH AMERICA
Its strong tail and webbed feet help the otter swim in search of fish and other prey.

Bullfrog
UNITED STATES
The largest North American frog, the bullfrog is a skillful hunter on land and in water.

Platypus
AUSTRALIA, TASMANIA
With the help of its sensitive ducklike bill, the platypus probes the mud of the riverbed for shellfish and insects.

Bream
EUROPE, NORTHERN ASIA
This fish feeds on the river bottom, using its tubelike mouth to gather insects, snails, and worms.

Ganges dolphin

FOUND IN:
India

SIZE:
5-8 ft

SCIENTIFIC NAME:
Platanista gangetica

One of only five freshwater dolphins, the Ganges dolphin lives in muddy rivers. It is blind and uses radarlike echolocation signals to find its prey.

Lechwe

FOUND IN:
Africa

SIZE:
body 4-5 ft;
tail 11-17 in

SCIENTIFIC NAME:
Kobus leche

The lechwe spends much of its time wading in shallow water, where it feeds on grasses and water plants.

Eurasian beaver

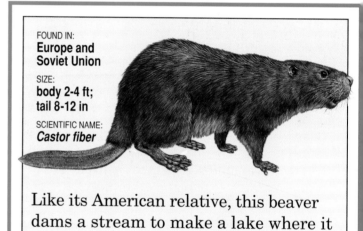

FOUND IN:
Europe and
Soviet Union

SIZE:
body 2-4 ft;
tail 8-12 in

SCIENTIFIC NAME:
Castor fiber

Like its American relative, this beaver dams a stream to make a lake where it stores its winter food supply of branches.

Australian water rat

Webbed hind feet make this large rodent a good swimmer. It feeds on small fish, frogs, and shellfish which it catches underwater.

FOUND IN:
Australia, Tasmania,
New Guinea

SIZE:
body 8-14 in;
tail 8-14 in

SCIENTIFIC NAME:
*Hydromys
chrysogaster*

Capybara

The largest living rodent, the capybara has webbed feet and is an excellent swimmer. It feeds on water plants.

FOUND IN:
South America

SIZE:
3-4 ft

SCIENTIFIC NAME:
Hydrochoerus hydrochaeris

Water opossum

The water opossum is the only marsupial, pouched animal, that lives in water.

FOUND IN:
Mexico, Central America, South America

SIZE:
body 10-13 in; tail 14-16 in

SCIENTIFIC NAME:
Chironectes minimus

Giant otter shrew

The otter shrew lives in a burrow in the riverbank with an entrance below water level. At night it enters the water to hunt prey such as crabs, fish, and frogs.

FOUND IN:
Africa

SIZE:
body 11-14 in; tail 9-11 in

SCIENTIFIC NAME:
Potomogale velox

Hippopotamus

The huge hippo swims and dives well, with the aid of its strong legs and webbed toes. It feeds on riverside plants.

FOUND IN:
Africa, south of the Sahara

SIZE:
body 9-14 ft; tail 14-20 in

SCIENTIFIC NAME:
Hippopotamus amphibius

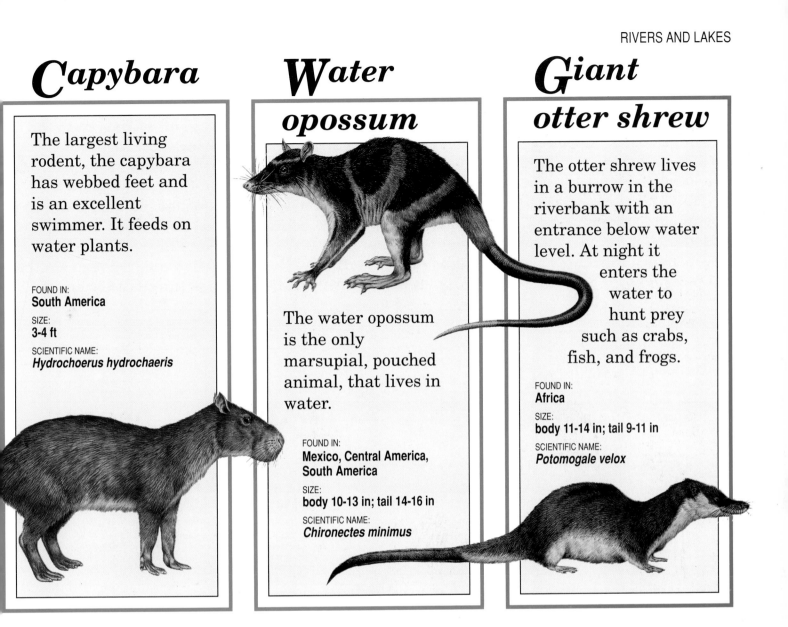

Focus on: *A European river*

By the time a river is nearing the sea, it is usually wide, deep, and flowing at a gentle pace. Its bottom is muddy and its water murky.

In Europe, rivers like these are full of life, especially in spring and summer when the plants on their banks and beneath the water are growing fast.

Animals, large and small, feed on the plants. Some fish, such as carp, pull at them under the surface; the mute swan dips its long neck under plants to nibble at them.

Small animals have many enemies in the rivers. The young of dragonflies seize tadpoles and even small fish such as sticklebacks in their strong jaws. Adult dragonflies dart over the water catching flying insects such as damselflies, their smaller cousins.

Most of the bigger animals that live in and around rivers also hunt for their food. Many fish can snatch insects and other small

Eurasian otter
An expert swimmer and diver, the otter pushes itself through the water with its thick tail and webbed feet.

Kingfisher
In the nesting season, a kingfisher pair makes a long tunnel in the riverbank, where the female lays her eggs.

Perch
Barred markings on the perch's body help camouflage it among water plants.

Common moorhen
A lively bird, the moorhen feeds on land and in water, taking pond weeds, berries, and some insects.

Mallard
This duck often feeds tail-up in shallow water. It eats plants and insects.

invertebrates, but the pike is powerful enough to drag water birds such as mallards from the surface.

Herons and kingfishers watch for passing fish from the riverbank, while the water shrew dives into the water and then drags its victims back to dry land before eating them.

Eel
Although eels live in rivers, they go to sea to lay their eggs. The young eels slowly drift back to the rivers.

Roach
This common river fish feeds on plants as well as on insects and other small creatures.

Northern pike
A fierce predator, the pike lurks among plants, keeping watch for any prey.

Water vole
A burrow dug in the riverbank is the home of this vole. It feeds on grasses and other plants.

91

Great crested grebe

These birds are famous for their courtship dance. Holding waterweed in their beaks, the male and female birds swim together, then rear up out of the water, swinging their heads from side to side.

FOUND IN:
Europe, Asia, East and South Africa, Australia, New Zealand

SIZE:
20 in

SCIENTIFIC NAME:
Podiceps cristatus

Great white pelican

FOUND IN:
Northern Europe, Africa, Asia

SIZE:
4-6 ft

SCIENTIFIC NAME:
Pelecanus onocrotalus

Pelicans normally fish in a group. Swimming in a wide circle, they herd schools of fish into the center and scoop them into their throat pouches.

Dipper

This little bird lives around mountain streams. It can swim underwater and even walks on the bottom to find insects and other small prey.

FOUND IN:
North America

SIZE:
7-8 in

SCIENTIFIC NAME:
Cinclus mexicanus

North American jacana

The jacana has extraordinarily long toes. These spread out its weight over such a large surface that it is actually able to walk on floating lily pads.

FOUND IN:
United States, Central America, Caribbean

SIZE:
10 in

SCIENTIFIC NAME:
Jacana spinosa

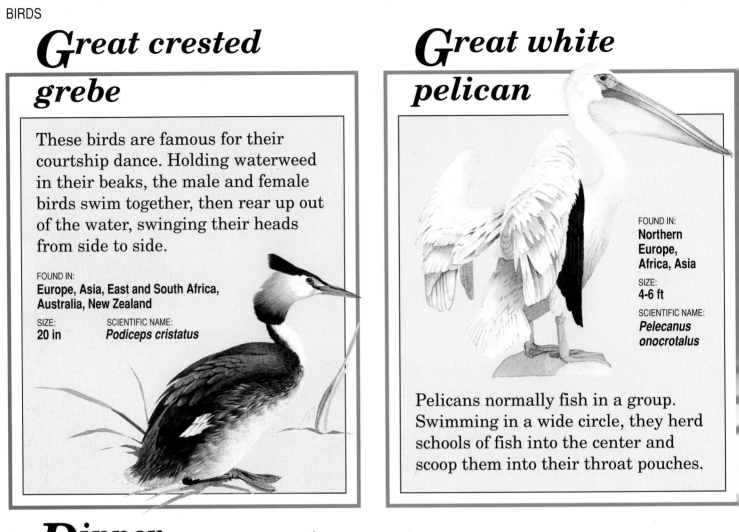

Mandarin duck

The beautiful mandarin duck feeds on seeds, acorns, and rice as well as insects, snails, and small fish.

FOUND IN:
Eastern Asia, China, Japan; introduced in ponds and lakes worldwide

SIZE:
17-20 in

SCIENTIFIC NAME:
Aix galericulata

Torrent tyrannulet

This bird lives by fast-flowing streams. It often plucks insects from slippery rocks surrounded by foaming water, drenching itself in the process.

FOUND IN:
Central and South America

SIZE:
4 in

SCIENTIFIC NAME:
Serpophaga cinerea

Limpkin

FOUND IN:
United States, Mexico, Caribbean, Central America

SIZE:
23-28 in

SCIENTIFIC NAME:
Aramus guarauna

This long-legged wading bird uses its curved beak to probe for snails and mussels in muddy swamps. It is called the limpkin because it seems to limp when it walks.

Osprey

FOUND IN:
almost worldwide

SIZE:
21-24 in

SCIENTIFIC NAME:
Pandion haliaetus

The osprey feeds on fish, plunging into the water feet first to seize its prey. Spines on the soles of its feet help the osprey hold onto the slippery fish.

Spotted water snake

FOUND IN:
Australia

SIZE:
12-20 in

SCIENTIFIC NAME:
Enhydris punctata

Able to move swiftly in water
and on land, this snake has
special pads of skin which
close its nostrils when it dives.

Oriental fire-bellied toad

The brilliantly
colored skin of this
toad gives off a milky
substance which
irritates the mouth
and eyes of any
attacker.

FOUND IN:
Soviet Union, China

SIZE:
2 in

SCIENTIFIC NAME:
Bombina orientalis

Hellbender

During the day this large salamander hides under
rocks in the water. At night it comes out to hunt
crayfish, snails, and worms, which it finds
by smell and touch rather than sight.

FOUND IN:
United States

SIZE:
12-29 in

SCIENTIFIC NAME:
Cryptobranchus alleganiensis

Alligator snapping turtle

This turtle rests on the riverbed,
with its large mouth open to show
a pink fleshy flap on its lower
jaw. Passing fish come to try this
"bait" and are quickly swallowed
by the turtle.

FOUND IN:
United States

SIZE:
13-26 in

SCIENTIFIC NAME:
*Macroclemys
temmincki*

Gavial

The gavial has long jaws studded with about 100 small teeth—ideal equipment for seizing fish and frogs underwater. Like all crocodiles, the gavial has been hunted for its skin and is now rare.

FOUND IN:
India

SIZE:
23 ft

SCIENTIFIC NAME:
Gavialis gangeticus

Warty newt

A large, rough-skinned newt, the male develops a jagged crest on his back in the breeding season. The female does not have a crest.

FOUND IN:
Europe

SIZE:
5-7 in

SCIENTIFIC NAME:
Triturus cristatus

Common frog

Much of this frog's life is spent on land, feeding on insects, spiders, and other small creatures. It mates in water, where the female lays as many as 4,000 eggs.

FOUND IN:
Europe

SIZE:
up to 4 in

SCIENTIFIC NAME:
Rana temporaria

Matamata

Camouflaged by its strange shape, this turtle lies on the riverbed, waiting to swallow passing fish.

FOUND IN:
Northern South America

SIZE:
16 in

SCIENTIFIC NAME:
Chelus fimbriatus

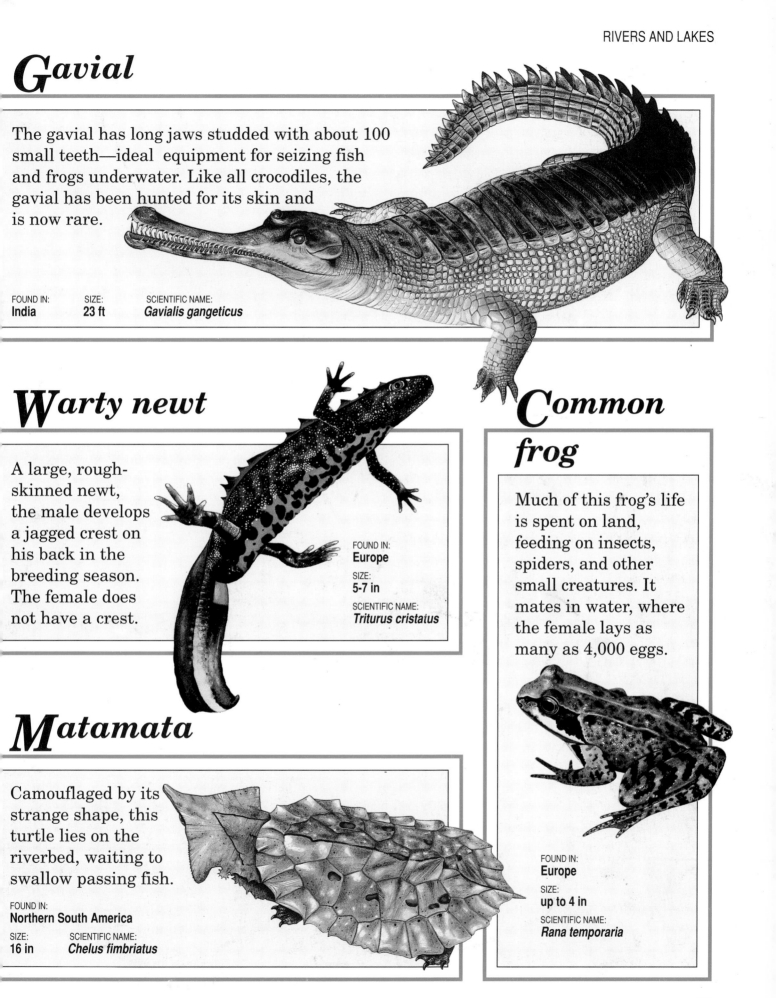

Electric eel

Special muscles in the electric eel's body release high-voltage electric charges into the water. The eel uses these shocks to kill prey, usually fish, or to defend itself from enemies. The charge can even give a human a severe shock.

FOUND IN:
South America

SIZE:
8 ft

SCIENTIFIC NAME:
Electrophorus electricus

Rainbow trout

The rainbow trout feeds mainly on shellfish and insect young. It is farmed in large quantities as a food fish.

FOUND IN:
Western North America; introduced worldwide

SIZE:
up to 3 ft

SCIENTIFIC NAME:
Salmo gairdneri

Brown bullhead

The bullhead lives on the muddy bottom of ponds and rivers, where it feeds on plants and fish.

FOUND IN:
North America; introduced in Europe and New Zealand

SIZE:
11-18 in

SCIENTIFIC NAME:
Ictalurus nebulosus

Nile perch

FOUND IN:
Africa

SIZE:
6-7 ft

SCIENTIFIC NAME:
Lates niloticus

This large, plump perch feeds mostly on smaller fish. It is an important food fish in Africa.

Paddlefish

The paddlefish swims with its large mouth open and its lower jaw dropped. Any small creatures in the water are caught on comblike structures in the fish's mouth.

FOUND IN:
United States

SIZE:
6-7 ft

SCIENTIFIC NAME:
Polyodon spathula

Red piranha

Armed with their strong jaws and razor-sharp teeth, piranhas hunt in groups and can kill prey larger than themselves.

FOUND IN:
Northern South America

SIZE:
up to 12 in

SCIENTIFIC NAME:
Serrasalmus nattereri

Angelfish

FOUND IN:
South America

SIZE:
6 in

SCIENTIFIC NAME:
Pterophyllum scalare

In the wild the angelfish lives in muddy, plant-filled water, where its flattened body and long fins, with trailing threadlike structures, keep it camouflaged. Angelfish are popular aquarium fish.

African lungfish

Unlike most fish, which breathe through gills, the lungfish has special lungs that allow it to breathe air at the water surface. In a long dry period, it can survive without water in a deep burrow in the lake or riverbed.

FOUND IN:
East and Central Africa

SIZE:
6 ft

SCIENTIFIC NAME:
Protopterus aethiopicus

97

Oceans

More than two-thirds of the Earth is covered with seawater, which provides homes for millions of animals

As everybody knows, the sea is salty. This is because it contains lots of dissolved minerals, many of them brought down from the land by rivers. When a river meets the sea, its fresh water mixes with the salty seawater. The river is usually very wide at this stage and is known as an estuary.

On either side of a river mouth runs the seashore. Some shores are rocky, with steep cliffs and underwater boulders. Here the waves pound against the land. Other shores have broad sandy or pebbly beaches where the waves are much more gentle. Tides make the sea rise and fall, so parts of the shore are only under water some of the time. Away from the shore, on the open sea, waves and tides are not so important. The surface may be rough but the water is calm only a few yards below.

Seawater may look clear, but it is actually teeming with plants. These are not the leafy plants of the land but tiny plants called plankton which can be seen only through a microscope. The plankton floats about, soaking up the sunshine in the surface waters. It grows best in places where deep ocean currents stir up the water, bringing lots of minerals and other plant food up from the seabed. Many sea creatures feed on plant plankton.

Where the sea is not too deep, usually close to land, sunlight can reach the bottom and plenty of seaweed can grow. Most seaweed does not float like plankton but is anchored among the sand and rocks of the seabed.

Farther out to sea, where the water is very deep, hardly any light reaches the seabed. At depths of about 600 feet, it is always gloomy. Below this, there may be thousands of feet of seawater, and here it is too dark for any plants—plankton or seaweed—to grow. The only living things that are found in these ocean depths are animals.

Perfectly designed for life in water, New Zealand fur seals dive deep below the surface in search of fish to eat.

Life in the oceans

As well as the many kinds of fishes in the sea, there are whales, seals, turtles, seabirds, shellfish, starfish, crabs, shrimp, worms, jellyfish, and tiny animal plankton. Some move about just by floating in the currents; others crawl on the bottom or swim through the water using their fins and flippers.

Most sea creatures take their oxygen from the surrounding water. But mammals, birds, and reptiles that dive into and swim in the sea have to come to the surface to breathe. They are much better at holding their breath than we are. Some whales can stay under water for more than an hour.

Sea animals find their food in many different ways. Plant and animal plankton are the most important sources of food and many creatures, large and small, swallow them as they swim

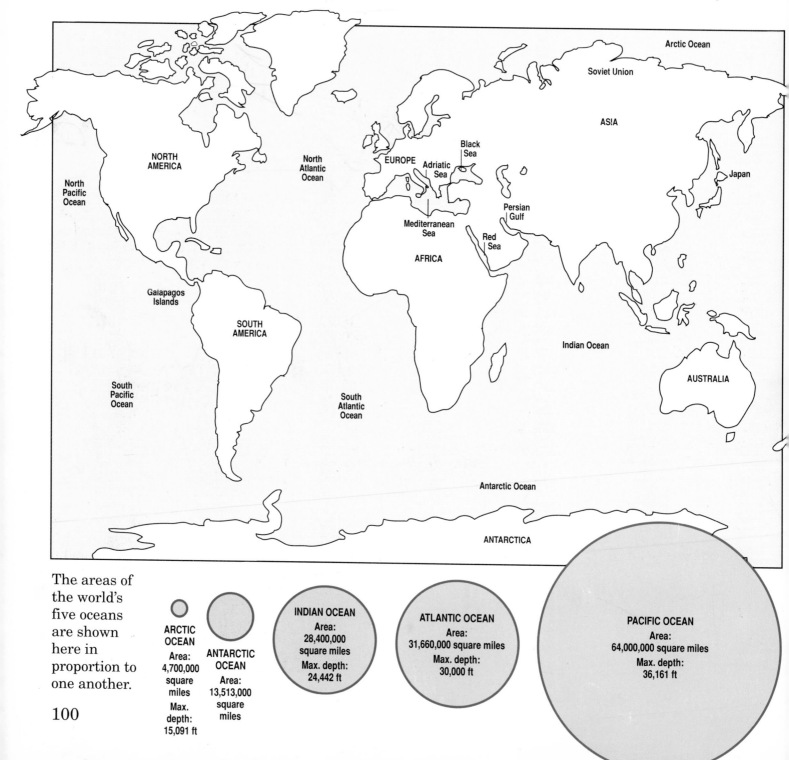

The areas of the world's five oceans are shown here in proportion to one another.

ARCTIC OCEAN
Area: 4,700,000 square miles
Max. depth: 15,091 ft

ANTARCTIC OCEAN
Area: 13,513,000 square miles

INDIAN OCEAN
Area: 28,400,000 square miles
Max. depth: 24,442 ft

ATLANTIC OCEAN
Area: 31,660,000 square miles
Max. depth: 30,000 ft

PACIFIC OCEAN
Area: 64,000,000 square miles
Max. depth: 36,161 ft

or float near the surface.
  Hunting animals seize prey with their tentacles or in their jaws. In deep sea it is very dark and gloomy and hunters have to use hearing, smell, and sight to find their victims. Many can tell what is near by sensing any movements in the water.

Leatherback
ALL OCEANS
The largest turtle in the world, the leatherback swims with the aid of its long, powerful front flippers. It feeds mainly on jellyfish.

Common dolphin
PACIFIC OCEAN, ATLANTIC OCEAN, INDIAN OCEAN
When it dives in search of fish and squid, the dolphin can go down as far as 1,000 feet below the surface of the sea.

Common puffin
NORTH ATLANTIC OCEAN
The puffin's large bill allows it to carry several fish back to its nest.

Swordfish
PACIFIC OCEAN, ATLANTIC OCEAN, INDIAN OCEAN
A fierce hunter, the swordfish has a streamlined body to help it move swiftly through the water.

Lionfish
INDIAN OCEAN, PACIFIC OCEAN
This brightly colored fish defends itself with the poisonous spines on its back fin.

Californian sea lion
PACIFIC COAST OF NORTH AMERICA
Agile in water, the sea lion can also move fast on land by tucking its back flippers forward under its body.

101

Killer whale

FOUND IN:
coastal waters worldwide

SIZE:
23-32 ft

SCIENTIFIC NAME:
Orcinus orca

Killer whales are fierce hunters and feed on fish, squid, sea lions, birds, and even other whales. They live and hunt in family groups.

Dugong

FOUND IN:
coastal waters of East Africa and from Red Sea to northern Australia

SIZE:
up to 10 ft

SCIENTIFIC NAME:
Dugong dugon

A shy, solitary animal, the dugong spends much of its life on the seabed, feeding on seaweed and sea grass.

Atlantic bottle-nosed dolphin

These dolphins live in groups of up to 15 animals. They feed mainly on fish.

FOUND IN:
warm and tropical seas worldwide

SIZE:
10-14 ft

SCIENTIFIC NAME:
Tursiops truncatus

Northern elephant seal

FOUND IN:
Pacific coast of North America

SIZE:
up to 20 ft

SCIENTIFIC NAME:
Mirounga angustirostris

The huge male elephant seal may weigh up to 6,000 pounds—as much as 40 people.

Blue whale

FOUND IN:
all oceans

SIZE:
82-105 ft

SCIENTIFIC NAME:
Balaenoptera musculus

Humpback whale

Humpbacks keep in touch and attract mates by singing long, complex songs.

FOUND IN:	SIZE:	SCIENTIFIC NAME:
all oceans	48-62 ft	*Megaptera novaeangliae*

Harbor seal

Like all seals, the harbor seal spends most of its life in water, coming to land only to mate and give birth. It feeds mainly on fish and squid.

FOUND IN:	SIZE:	SCIENTIFIC NAME:
coastal waters of North Atlantic and North Pacific oceans	4-6 ft	*Phoca vitulina*

Harbor porpoise

FOUND IN:
North Atlantic and North Pacific oceans; Mediterranean and Black seas

SIZE: 4-6 ft SCIENTIFIC NAME: *Phocoena phocoena*

Porpoises feed on fish, such as herring and mackerel, and can dive for up to six minutes when hunting prey.

The largest mammal that has ever lived, the blue whale may weigh more than 160 tons. This giant feeds on huge quantities of tiny shrimplike creatures called krill.

Red-tailed tropicbird

FOUND IN:
Indian and Pacific oceans

SIZE:
body 16 in; tail 20 in

SCIENTIFIC NAME:
Phaethon rubricauda

This elegant, fast-flying seabird feeds mainly on fish and squid. It is a poor swimmer and often catches its prey by hovering above the water, then plunging down to seize its victim. It usually makes its nest on a cliff ledge in a position for easy takeoff.

Razorbill

The razorbill swims well and dives from the surface to catch prey such as fish and shellfish in its strong bill. Razorbills nest in large groups on sea cliffs and rocky shores.

FOUND IN:
North Atlantic Ocean

SIZE:
16-17 in

SCIENTIFIC NAME:
Alca torda

Wandering albatross

The longest-winged of any bird, the albatross soars over the open ocean, sometimes covering as much as 300 miles a day. It alights on the sea to feed on fish, squid, and food refuse from ships.

FOUND IN:
Southern oceans

SIZE:
42-53 in; wingspan 114-128 in

SCIENTIFIC NAME:
Diomedea exulans

Kittiwake

The kittiwake builds its nest on a high cliff ledge from plants, seaweed, guano, and mud. The female lays two eggs.

FOUND IN:
Northern Pacific and Atlantic oceans; Arctic Ocean

SIZE:
16-18 in

SCIENTIFIC NAME:
Rissa tridactyla

Great cormorant

Using its webbed feet to push itself through the water and its long tail for steering, the cormorant catches fish under water. Its hunting dives last up to a minute, and it usually brings prey back to the surface for eating.

FOUND IN:
North Atlantic, Africa, Europe, Asia, Australia

SIZE:
31-39 in

SCIENTIFIC NAME:
Phalacrocorax carbo

Wilson's petrel

FOUND IN:
Antarctic, Atlantic, Indian oceans

SIZE:
6-7 in

SCIENTIFIC NAME:
Oceanites oceanicus

This petrel hops and paddles over the surface of the water picking up prey. It also feeds on refuse thrown from ships.

Galapagos penguin

Like all penguins, this bird cannot fly but catches fish and squid under water.

FOUND IN:
Galapagos Islands

SIZE:
20 in

SCIENTIFIC NAME:
Spheniscus mendiculus

Northern gannet

FOUND IN:
North Atlantic Ocean

SIZE:
34-39 in

SCIENTIFIC NAME:
Sula bassana

This seabird soars over the ocean, searching for fish and squid. When it spots prey, the gannet makes a rapid dive and grasps the catch in its strong, sharp bill.

Focus on: *Pacific deep sea*

Far out in the middle of the ocean the water is unimaginably deep. The deepest part of the Pacific Ocean is more than 35,000 feet under water. Below about 3,000 feet there is no sunlight, the temperature is only just above freezing, and the weight of the water above is enough to crush most animals.

The body fluids of deep-sea creatures are kept at high pressure so even the most delicate ones, such as shrimp and jellyfish, are not crushed. They can also live in cold water without coming to harm. In the complete darkness, animals have to use senses other than sight to find their way around and detect danger. Many deep-sea fish can sense the slightest movements in the water around them.

It is hard for animals to find enough to eat in the deep sea. Plants cannot grow there and there is little animal plankton. Because food is scarce, most of the fish are small but have big, gaping mouths so they can trap any smaller animals that come within reach.

Some creatures, such as shrimp, crawl over the muddy bottom, searching for fragments of dead plants and animals that drift down from the waters above.

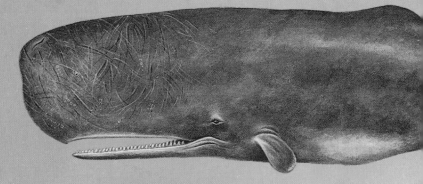

Sperm whale
A champion diver, the sperm whale often dives down to 3,000 feet to find fish and squid to eat.

Oarfish
This strange fish has a flattened ribbonlike body and can grow as long as 23 feet. It feeds on small shrimp.

Linophryne arborifera
Prey are attracted to the luminous "fishing rod" lure on the nose of this tiny fish. Once a victim is within reach, *Linophryne* snaps it up.

Gulper eel
Its huge jaws gaping, this eel swims through the water and swallows any fish that stray into its open mouth.

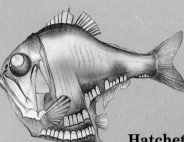

Hatchetfish
Rows of light-producing organs on the belly help hatchetfish recognize each other in the deep, dark sea.

Atelopus japonicus
This slender, fragile fish is thought to feed on worms, crabs, and other creatures on the seabed.

Slender snipe eel
With the help of its long beaklike jaws, this eel catches prey such as crabs and fish.

Sloane's viperfish
An extension of the back fin of this fish makes a lure to attract prey. The victim is then seized in the viperfish's fanglike teeth.

Atlantic manta

FOUND IN:
coastal waters of Atlantic Ocean

SIZE:
17 ft long; 22 ft wide

SCIENTIFIC NAME:
Manta birostris

Like many of the ocean giants, the Atlantic manta feeds on tiny animal plankton which it filters from the water. It also eats fish and large shellfish.

Green turtle

The green turtle spends most of its life in water, feeding on seaweed and sea grasses. It may travel hundreds of miles to lay its eggs on the beach where it was born.

FOUND IN:
warm waters of all oceans

SIZE:
3-4 ft

SCIENTIFIC NAME:
Chelonia mydas

Sandy dogfish

This slender fish is actually a small shark. It feeds on shellfish and worms which it finds on the seabed.

FOUND IN:
coastal waters of eastern North Atlantic

SIZE:
23-40 in

SCIENTIFIC NAME:
Scyliorhinus canicula

Marine iguana

FOUND IN:
Galapagos Islands

SIZE:
4-5 ft

SCIENTIFIC NAME:
Amblyrhynchus cristatus

At home on land and in the sea, this iguana swims and dives with ease as it searches for seaweed, its main food. It uses its strong tail to push itself along in water.

White shark

FOUND IN:
warm and tropical coastal waters of Atlantic, Pacific, and Indian oceans

SIZE:
up to 20 ft

SCIENTIFIC NAME:
Cacharodon carcharias

One of the fiercest hunters in the sea, the white shark feeds on seals, dolphins, and fish—even other sharks.

Estuarine crocodile

This large and dangerous crocodile spends most of its life in the sea, hunting fish. It lays its eggs on land.

FOUND IN:
coastal waters and estuaries from India to Australia

SIZE:
up to 20 ft

SCIENTIFIC NAME:
Crocodylus porosus

Smooth hammerhead

FOUND IN:
warm and tropical waters of Atlantic, Pacific, and Indian oceans

SIZE:
14 ft

SCIENTIFIC NAME:
Sphyrna zygaena

This shark's head has long lobes on each side bearing its eyes and nostrils. No one knows why the head is this shape but it may help the shark see and smell.

Banded sea snake

FOUND IN:
coastal waters of Persian Gulf, Indian Ocean, Pacific Ocean to Japan

SIZE:
6-7 ft

SCIENTIFIC NAME:
Hydrophis cyanocinctus

This snake spends all its life in the sea and never comes to land. It feeds mainly on fish and is extremely poisonous.

Conger eel

John Dory

FOUND IN :
coastal waters of North Atlantic Ocean

SIZE:
9 ft

SCIENTIFIC NAME:
Conger conger

A stealthy hunter, the John Dory swims slowly toward its prey until it is close enough to seize it in its huge mouth.

FOUND IN:
Atlantic Ocean and Mediterranean Sea

SIZE:
15-26 in

SCIENTIFIC NAME:
Zeus faber

The conger eel is common on Atlantic shores. It usually lives in shallow water, often close to rocks, and feeds mainly on fish, crabs, and octopus. It travels to deeper water to lay its eggs.

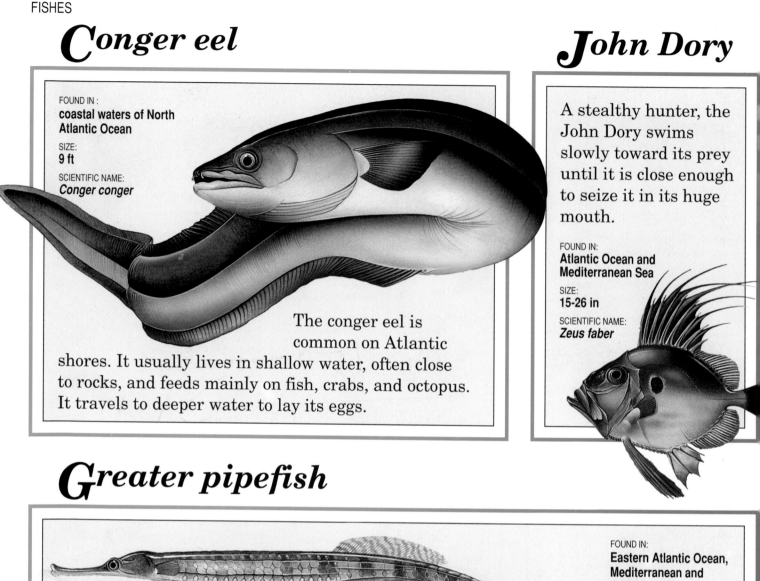

Greater pipefish

Pipefish breed in the summer months. The male incubates the eggs in a special pouch under the tail. Fully formed young hatch out from the pouch after about five weeks.

FOUND IN:
Eastern Atlantic Ocean, Mediterranean and Adriatic seas

SIZE:
12-18 in

SCIENTIFIC NAME:
Syngnathus acus

Bluefish

An extremely fierce hunter, the bluefish kills and eats almost any other fish, including young of its own species.

FOUND IN:
warm and tropical waters of Atlantic, Indian, and western Pacific oceans

SIZE:
up to 4 ft

SCIENTIFIC NAME:
Pomatomus saltatrix

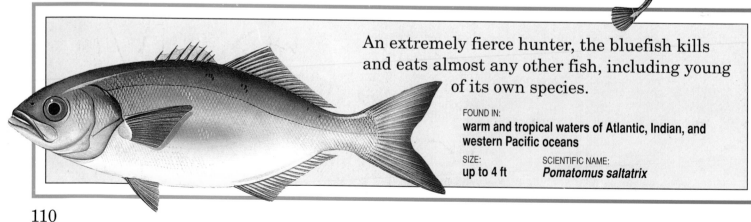

Atlantic cod

Cod usually swim in schools in surface waters but will search for food such as fish and worms on the seabed.

FOUND IN:
coastal waters of North Atlantic Ocean

SIZE:
4 ft

SCIENTIFIC NAME:
Gadus morhua

Sharksucker

On top of this fish's flattened head is a strong sucking disk which it uses to attach itself to the body of a larger animal. Thus the sharksucker gets a free ride and protection.

FOUND IN:
tropical waters of Atlantic, Indian, and western Pacific oceans

SIZE:
up to 36 in

SCIENTIFIC NAME:
Echenis naucrates

Atlantic flyingfish

With its winglike fins held out, this fish can rise above the surface of the water and glide along for up to 300 feet. It usually "flies" in this way to escape enemies.

FOUND IN:
Atlantic Ocean and Mediterranean Sea

SIZE:
12-17 in

SCIENTIFIC NAME:
Cypselurus heterurus

Herring

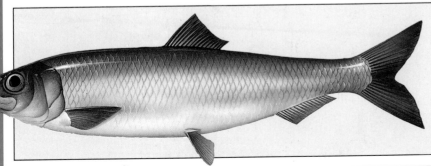

The herring feeds mainly on tiny animal plankton but also eats small fish and shellfish.

FOUND IN:
North Atlantic Ocean

SIZE:
16 in

SCIENTIFIC NAME:
Clupea harengus

Focus on: *Great Barrier Reef*

Australia's Great Barrier Reef is home to at least 3,000 different kinds of animals. There are sponges, jellyfish, shrimp, sea anemones, octopus, crabs, and starfish, as well as an amazing variety of fish.

Most coral reefs are in shallow water near the coasts of warm, tropical seas. These conditions best suit the coral animals—the small creatures that build hard, stony chambers of coral around themselves for protection.

Corals live in great colonies so this stony material builds up over time to make large reefs. The Great Barrier Reef off the coast of Australia is the largest in the world at more than 1,200 miles long.

There is plenty of food available for the animals that live on the reef. Some fish, starfish, and worms eat the living coral. Sponges attach themselves to the reef and filter tiny bits of food from the water. Lots of animals, including some of the corals, trap or catch small prey, and the biggest predators such as sharks hunt large fish.

The fish that live on coral reefs are extremely colorful. Their colors probably help them recognize members of their own species among all the others. But against the bright corals, some of the patterns can also provide good camouflage when predators are about.

Mandarinfish
In the wild this fish lives on the seabed among rocks or coral. It is also a popular aquarium species.

Great barracuda
An expert hunter, the barracuda catches other fish with the help of its large mouth studded with long, sharp teeth.

Imperial angelfish
This prettily patterned fish feeds on the coral animals themselves.

Stonefish
Needlelike spines on the stonefish's back contain a poison so deadly it can even kill a human.

Hawksbill
This turtle feeds on crabs and other shellfish on rocky coasts and reefs.

Batfish
Its flattened body helps this fish move around the nooks and crannies of the reef.

Copperband butterflyfish
With the help of its long beaklike snout, this fish reaches into crevices in the coral to find food.

Blue-spotted boxfish
The body of this fish is covered with a shell of bony plates which protect it from enemies.

Sweetlip emperor
This colorful, heavy-bodied fish is one of the hunters on the reef.

113

Moorish idol

FOUND IN:
shallow waters of Indian and Pacific oceans

SIZE:
7 in

SCIENTIFIC NAME:
Zanclus cornutus

The tubelike mouth of this brightly colored fish helps it feed in the crevices of coral reefs.

Ocean sunfish

This unusual fish has an almost circular body ending in a frill-like tail. It feeds mainly on tiny animal plankton.

FOUND IN:
warm and tropical waters of Atlantic, Pacific, and Indian oceans

SIZE:
up to 13 ft

SCIENTIFIC NAME:
Mola mola

Plaice

FOUND IN:
shallow waters of eastern Atlantic Ocean and Mediterranean Sea

SIZE:
20-36 in

SCIENTIFIC NAME:
Pleuronectes platessa

A bottom-living fish, the plaice lies on the seabed feeding on worms, crabs, and other shellfish.

Rainbow parrotfish

This colorful fish has strong beaklike jaws which it uses to scrape seaweed and coral off reefs to eat. Large grinding teeth farther back in its mouth crush the food.

FOUND IN:
coastal waters and coral reefs in western Atlantic Ocean

SIZE:
up to 4 ft

SCIENTIFIC NAME:
Scarus guacamaia

Icefish

FOUND IN:
shallow waters of Antarctic Ocean

SIZE:
24 in

SCIENTIFIC NAME:
Chaenocephalus aceratus

The long, slender icefish has beaklike jaws. It spends much of its time close to the seabed, feeding on fish and shellfish.

Clown triggerfish

If alarmed, this fish hides in a crevice and wedges itself in with a spine on its back. This spine is locked into an upright position by a second spine, making the fish very hard to move.

FOUND IN:
rocky coasts and coral reefs in Indian and Pacific oceans

SIZE:
13 in

SCIENTIFIC NAME:
Balistoides conspicillum

Clown anemonefish

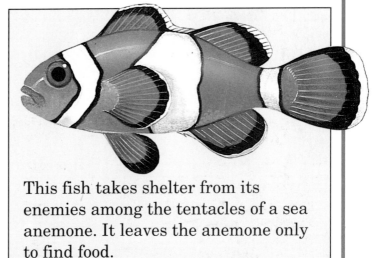

This fish takes shelter from its enemies among the tentacles of a sea anemone. It leaves the anemone only to find food.

FOUND IN:
Western and central Pacific Ocean

SIZE:
2 in

SCIENTIFIC NAME:
Amphiprion percula

Yellowfin tuna

Like all tuna, the yellowfin has a streamlined body and is a fast-swimming hunter. It feeds mainly on fish and squid.

FOUND IN:
warm and tropical waters worldwide

SIZE:
6 ft

SCIENTIFIC NAME:
Thunnus albacares

115

GLOSSARY

You may find it useful to know the scientific meanings of these words when reading this book.

Amphibian: A cold-blooded animal that can live in both land and water. There are about 2,000 species which include newts, salamanders, frogs, and toads. Amphibians lay eggs from which their young hatch.

Bird: A warm-blooded animal covered with feathers. There are about 8,600 species of birds. All birds have wings and most can fly. They lay eggs in which their young develop until they are ready to hatch.

Carnivore: An animal that feeds on meat.

Coral: Undersea rock made by many minute creatures related to jellyfish. Each creature, or coral polyp, makes a hard covering for itself. When enough of these are combined together, a coral reef forms.

Evergreen: Describes a plant (usually a tree or shrub) that does not lose all its leaves at one season of the year.

Fish: An animal that lives in water and has fins instead of legs. There are more than 20,000 species. Fish breathe through gills, not lungs, and most lay eggs.

Habitat: The place where an animal or plant lives.

Herbivore: An animal that feeds only on plants.

Mammal: A warm-blooded animal, usually four-legged and hairy, that gives birth to fully formed young. Female mammals feed their young on milk from their mammary glands. There are about 4,000 species of mammals.

Migration: The regular movement of a group of animals from one area to another.

Plankton: The minute plants and animals suspended in the ocean or in fresh water. Many creatures feed on plankton.

Predator: An animal that hunts and kills other animals for food.

Prey: The animals hunted by predators.

Reptile: A cold-blooded, scaly skinned animal. There are about 6,000 species which include turtles, tortoises, lizards, crocodiles, and snakes.

Rodent: An animal in the order of mammals called Rodentia, which includes rats, mice, and squirrels.

Scavenger: A creature that feeds on the remains of animals that have died naturally or have been killed by predators.

Species: A term for a type of plant or animal. Living things of the same species can mate and produce young which can themselves have young. Animals or plants of different species cannot do this.

Subtropical: Describes parts of the world that border on tropical areas but are not hot enough to be tropical.

Temperate: Regions of the world that are moderate in their climate, with clearly defined summer and winter seasons.

Tropical: The hot, wet regions of the world around the equator.

NDEX

A

der, puff 44

saw-scaled 60

gamid, Arabian
   toad-headed 60

laska 8

batross, wandering 104

nphibians and reptiles
   36-37, 48-49, 60-61,
   74-75, 94-95

iaconda 87

iemonefish, clown 115

igelfish 97
   imperial 112

iole, green 37

ntarctic 8

iteater, giant 41

itechinus, brown 32

itelope 40, 44, 52, 64

rctic 8

elopus japonicus 107

B

boon, olive 43

idger, Eurasian 29

rracuda, great 112

t, Queensland
   blossom 33

teleur 45

tfish 113

ar 22
   black 23
   brown 19, 84

aver 20
   Eurasian 88

rd of paradise, blue 65

rds 12-13, 24-25, 34-35,
   46-47, 58-59, 72-73,
   80-81, 92-93, 104-105

son 38, 43

iefish 110

ietail, red-flanked 24

a constrictor 74

a, emerald tree 65

boar, wild 31

bongo 71

boomslang 48

boxfish, blue-spotted 113

bream 87

buffalo 40

bullfrog 87

bullhead, brown 96

bunting, snow 15

bustard, great 41

butterfly 68

butterflyfish,
   copperband 113

C

cacti 56

camel 52
   bactrian 53

capercaillie, western 25

capybara 89

cardinal 35

caribou 10, 13, 22

cat, Pallas's 54

chamois 80

cheetah 41, 44

chickadee,
   black-capped 22

chinchilla-rat 79

chipmunk, eastern 30

chuckwalla 60

coati 70

cockatoo 32
   sulfur-crested 33

cod, Atlantic 111

condor 78
   Andean 79

coniferous forests 16-25
   climate of 18
   in Canada 22-23
   map of 18

conifers 16

coquette, frilled 72

coral 112-113

cormorant, great 105

cottontail, desert 57

courser, cream-colored 53

creeper, brown 34

crocodile, estuarine 109

crossbill 19

cuckoo, African
   emerald 73

D

deciduous trees 26

deer 64
   white-tailed 30

deserts 50-61
   American Southwest
      56-57
   climate of 52
   map of 50
   plants in 50, 56

dipper 92

dog, hunting 44

dogfish, sandy 108

dolphin, Atlantic
   bottle-nosed 102
   common 101
   Ganges 88

dormouse 55

dove, mourning 56

dovekie 12

dragonflies 86, 90

duck, mandarin 93

dugong 102

E

eagle 22, 41, 78
   golden 79, 82
   harpy 69

eel 91
   conger 110
   electric 96
   gulper 106
   slender snipe 107

elephant, African 44, 45
   Indian 70

emperor, sweetlip 113

ermine 14

eucalyptus trees 32

F

finch, snow 79
   zebra 59

fishes 96-97, 108-111,
   114-115

flycatcher, vermilion 59

flyingfish, Atlantic 111

forest, coniferous 16-25
   tropical 62-75

fox 41
   Arctic 15
   fennec 53
   red 31

frog 86
   bullfrog 87
   common 95
   golden arrow-poison 74
   horned 69
   marsupial 75
   South African rain 48
   termite 49
   Wallace's flying 75

fruit bat, tube-nosed 66

G

gannet, northern 105

gavial 95

gazelle 53

gecko, leaf-tailed 74
   web-footed 61

gerbil, fat-tailed 53

gibbon, lar 66

gila monster 57

giraffe 40, 41, 44

glider, greater 33

goat 82

goat, mountain 69

gorilla 62, 66

goshawk 24
grasslands 38-49
    African 44-45
    climate of 40
    map of 40
grebe, great crested 92
grosbeak, pine 25
grouse, black 25
guineafowl, helmeted 45
gull, ivory 12
gyrfalcon 15

H
hammerhead, smooth 109
hare, Arctic 15
hatchetfish 107
hawk 18, 41
    Cooper's 35
    red-tailed 58
hawksbill 113
hedgehog, desert 55
hellbender 94
heron 91
    gray 87
herring 111
Himalayas 82-83
hippopotamus 89
honeycreeper, purple 72
hornbill, great Indian 65
    southern ground 47
howler, red 67
hummingbird 68
    Costa's 56
hunting dog 44
hyena 44

I
ibex 78
ibisbill 82
ice caps 8-15
    climate of 10
    map of 10

icefish 115
iguana, common 75
    marine 108
impala 44
insects 18, 28, 32, 40, 52,
    56, 57, 65, 68, 86, 90

J
jacana,
    North American 92
jackal 44
jackrabbit,
    black-tailed 41
jaguar 71
jay 34
jellyfish 106, 112
John Dory 110
junco, dark-eyed 23
jungle runner 49

K
kangaroo, red 55
kingfisher 64, 86, 90
    beautiful paradise 73
kinglet,
    golden-crowned 24
kittiwake 104
koala 29, 32
kookaburra 32
kowari 54

L
lakes and rivers 84-97
    largest 86
lammergeier 83
lark, desert 58
leatherback 101
lechwe 88
lemming 10, 18
    Norway 12
lemur 64

Philippine flying 67
leopard 44
limpkin 93
Linophryne arborifera
    106
lion 42, 44
    mountain 81
lionfish 101
lizard 28, 52
    Arabian toad-headed
        agamid 60
    chuckwalla 60
    desert night 56
    frilled 36
    gila monster 57
    jungle runner 49
    lace monitor 32
    plated 45
    sandfish 60
    thorny devil 53
    Transvaal snake 48
    western blue-tongued
        skink 61
loris, slender 67
lory, rainbow 33
lungfish, African 97
lynx 18, 20, 22
lyrebird, superb 34

M
macaw, scarlet 65
mallard 90
mammals 12-13, 20-21,
    30-31, 42-43, 54-55,
    66-67, 70-71, 80-81,
    88-89, 102-103
mandarinfish 112
manta, Atlantic 108
marmoset 68
marmot, Himalayan 82
marsupials 55
marten 18, 22, 23
matamata 95
meerkat 55

monkey 64, 68
    black spider 68
    red howler 67
moorhen, common 90
moorish idol 114
moose 16, 22
mountains 76-83
    Himalayas 82-83
    map of 78
    plants on 76
    tallest 78
mouse, birch 20
    harvest 87
    wood 30
musk ox 10, 11

N
newt, warty 95
nuthatch, red-breasted 2

O
oarfish 106
ocean sunfish 114
oceans 98-115
    Great Barrier Reef
        112-113
    map of 100-101
    Pacific deep sea 106
ocelot 68
octopus 112
okapi 65
opossum, water 89
orangutan 65
oriole, northern 34
oryx 53,
    Arabian 54
osprey 93
ostrich 44, 46
otter 86
    Eurasian 90
    giant 87
otter shrew, giant 89

wl 18, 22
  burrowing 46
  elf 57
  great horned 23
  hawk 24
  long-eared 19
  snowy 11
  tawny 29
xpecker, yellow-billed 47

addlefish 97
anda, red 82
arrot 32, 68
  eclectus 73
  yellow-headed 68
arrotfish, rainbow 114
eafowl, Indian 72
eccary 56, 68
eper, spring 36
elican, great white 92
enguin, emperor 8, 11
  Galapagos 105
erch 90
  Nile 96
eregrine falcon 80
etrel, Wilson's 105
heasant 82
g 64
  bearded 71
ka, northern 81
ke, northern 91
pefish, greater 110
ranha, red 97
aice 114
ankton 98
atypus 87
over, golden 13
lar bear 10, 11
rcupine 22
rpoise, harbor 103
ssum 32
  brush-tailed 33
airie 38, 40

prairie chicken,
  greater 47
prairie dog 40
  black-tailed 43
ptarmigan, rock 14
puffin, common 101
python, carpet 32

Q
quail-thrush,
  cinnamon 58
quelea, red-billed 46

R
rabbit,
  desert cottontail 57
  pygmy 54
  snowshoe 21
raccoon 31
rainforest 62-75
  Amazon 68-69
  plants of 62
rat, bamboo 70
  kangaroo 57
razorbill 104
reptiles and amphibians
  36-37, 48-49, 60-61,
  74-75, 94-95, 108-109
rhinoceros, black 43
rivers and lakes 84-97
  European river 90-91
  plants in 84
roach 91
roadrunner, greater 56
rosella 32

S
sable 20
saiga 42
salamander, fire 37
  hellbender 94

red-backed 29
  tiger 49
sandfish 60
sandgrouse 53
  Pallas's 58
sapsucker,
  yellow-bellied 29
savanna 38, 40, 44-45
scrub-robin, Karroo 59
sea lion, Californian 101
seal 10
  harbor 103
  leopard 12
  New Zealand fur 98
  northern elephant 102
secretary bird 46
semidesert 50, 52
seriema, red-legged 47
serval 44
shark, white 109
sharksucker 111
sheathbill, snowy 13
sheep 82
  Dall 76
shrew, masked 30
shrimp 106, 112
Siberia 14-15
sidewinder 61
sittella, varied 33
skink, Great Plains 48
  western blue-tongued
  61
sloth, two-toed 66
snake 28
  anaconda 87
  banded sea 109
  boa constrictor 74
  carpet python 32
  eastern coral 36
  emerald tree boa 65
  gopher 49
  grass 37
  paradise tree 74
  sidewinder 61
  snail-eating 69
  spotted water 94

western blind 56
snowcock, Himalayan 82
solitaire, Andean 81
spadefoot, western 61
spiders 68
sponge 112
squirrel 28, 64
  gray 29
  ground 40
  Indian striped 70
  red 19
starfish 112
steppe 38, 40
stoat 14
stonefish 113
sunbird, scarlet-tufted
  malachite 80
swan, tundra 15
swordfish 101

T
tahr 83
tamandua 69
tamarin, golden lion 67
tapir 68
  Brazilian 68
thorny devil 53
tiger 71
toad, midwife 37
  oriental fire-bellied 94
  western spadefoot 61
tortoise, leopard 41
  Schweigger's
  hingeback 75
toucan 68
toucanet, spot-billed 73
tragopan, Temminck's 81
triggerfish, clown 115
tropical forest 62-75
  climate of 64
  map of 64
tropicbird, red-tailed 104
trout, rainbow 96
tuna, yellowfin 115

tundra 8-15
   climate of 10
   map of 10
   Siberian 14-15
turtle 36
   alligator snapping 94
   green 108
   hawksbill 113
   leatherback 101
   wood 36
tyrannulet, torrent 93

U
umbrellabird,
   Amazonian 69

V
verdin 56
vicuna 80
viperfish, Sloane's 107
vole 10, 18
vulture 44
   king 72
   lappet-faced 59

W
wallcreeper 83
walrus 11
warthog 44
water rat, Australian 88
water shrew 91

water vole 91
whale, blue 102-103
   humpback 103
   killer 102
   sperm 106
whimbrel 14
wildebeest, blue 45
wolf, gray 21
   maned 42
wolverine 13, 22
wombat 31
woodchuck 21
woodcock, American 35
woodlands 26-37
   Australia's eucalyptus
   32-33
   climate of 28

map of 28
woodpecker, black 19
   great spotted 35
   pileated 26
wren, cactus 53, 56
   superb blue 32

Y
yak 83

Z
zebra 44
   common 42

ACKNOWLEDGMENTS

Illustration credits

Animal illustrations by:
Graham Allen
Alan Male
Colin Newman
Michael Woods
and Norman Arlott, Keith Brewer, Chris Christoforou,
Malcolm Ellis, Denys Ovenden, Dick Twinney

Background illustrations on pages:
14-15, 22-23, 32-33, 44-45, 56-57, 68-69, 82-83, 90-91,
106-107, 112-113 by **John Davis**

Photographic credits

All the following photographs supplied by
Oxford Scientific Films:

8-9 Doug Allan; 14 David C. Fritts; 16-17 Tom Ulrich;
23 Stan Osolinski; 26-27 Ted Levin/Animals Animals;
38-39 Stan Osolinski; 44-45 Edwin Sadd;
50-51 Anthony Bannister; 57 Stan Osolinski;
62-63 Andrew Plumptre; 76-77 David C. Fritts/Animals Animals;
82 Mike Brown; 84-85 Warwick Johnson;
91 Hans Reinhard/Okapia; 106 Kim Westerskov; 113 Len Zell